"Julian, I'm the only one who knew the gun was here," she cried. Her body stiffened. She raised her head. "I know everything keeps pointing to me but I swear I didn't kill her. I swear it!"

Julian leaned forward and pressed a kiss onto her forehead.

"I know you didn't do it," he assured her. "But you weren't the only one who knew where the gun was. Someone else had to have known. And if you didn't tell anyone where you put it, then—"

"Then someone must have followed me."

Julian tried not to let his body tense. He nodded, gaze sweeping the trees around them.

"But why?" she asked into his chest.

More than anything Julian wished he could give her an answer. He wished he could make it all better. Assuage her worries and take her to bed and give her some pleasure in place of the pain that seemed to keep finding its way to her.

But, instead, he was about to invite more worry and pain.

CREDIBLE ALIBI

TYLER ANNE SNELL

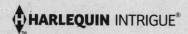
HARLEQUIN INTRIGUE®

This book is for Lissanne J., Marci M. and the Bat Signal crew.

Thank you for loving Madi and Julian and thank you for the
continued support, critique and constant hilarity.

This book is also for Madi Rice. I named a character after you
only to realize I never knew your real first name.

ISBN-13: 978-1-335-64098-7

Credible Alibi

Copyright © 2019 by Tyler Anne Snell

Recycling programs
for this product may
not exist in your area.

Printed in U.S.A.

Tyler Anne Snell genuinely loves all genres of the written word. However, she's realized that she loves books filled with sexual tension and mysteries a little more than the rest. Her stories have a good dose of both. Tyler lives in Alabama with her same-named husband and their mini "lions." When she isn't reading or writing, she's playing video games and working on her blog, *Almost There*. To follow her shenanigans, visit tylerannesnell.com.

Books by Tyler Anne Snell

Harlequin Intrigue

Winding Road Redemption

Reining in Trouble
Credible Alibi

The Protectors of Riker County

Small-Town Face-Off
The Deputy's Witness
Forgotten Pieces
Loving Baby
The Deputy's Baby
The Negotiation

Orion Security

Private Bodyguard
Full Force Fatherhood
Be on the Lookout: Bodyguard
Suspicious Activities

Manhunt

Visit the Author Profile page at Harlequin.com.

CAST OF CHARACTERS

Madeline Nash—As one of the Nash triplets abducted years ago, this innkeeper has lived with her life close to the chest. Yet after a handsome guest temporarily brings down her walls, she realizes her life will never be that simple again. Finding out she's pregnant with his child was unexpected, but finding herself framed for the murder of one of her guests months later is something no one saw coming. Now she's in dire need of protection. Lucky for her, the man she needs is already there.

Julian Mercer—After taking a detour to see the small-town innkeeper he can't get out of his head, this former marine finds that very same woman in the middle of chaos—and pregnant with his child. What was supposed to be a quick stop before starting his new life now has him doing anything to protect the new family he had no idea existed. Because while danger might be around every corner, it sure didn't count on him.

Loraine Wilson—Rich and deeply rude, this infuriating guest is found murdered at the inn with all fingers pointing at Madi.

Desmond and Caleb Nash—The brothers who make up the Nash triplets. The wealthy cowboy and detective do everything in their power to help clear their sister's name and keep her safe.

Dorothy Nash—The Nash family matriarch has seen her fair share of heartbreak but always reminds her children to stay optimistic.

Christian Miller—As the lead detective on the case, he has more bad blood with the Nash family than anyone else, promising he'll make sure Madi gets what's coming to her no matter the cost.

Chapter One

Julian Mercer didn't know this woman from Eve and yet he knew exactly three things about her the moment her baby blues swung his way.

One, she was hanging on to something that was heavy. As she made her way across the yard, following a path of mismatched stones embedded in the earth, there was an almost imperceptible drag to each step. Like there was an invisible weight on each shoulder that threw off a normal, happy gait. She was thinking of something and that something was difficult, whatever it was. Her polite, welcoming smile, which was required as the owner of the bed-and-breakfast, even had a tightness about it.

Two, someone or something had hurt her. Not just physically—though Julian clocked the small but noticeable scar that broke the smoothness of her skin above the left cheekbone. In addition to the subtle, weighted steps she took toward him, there was a hesitation. So small, yet he was as sure as his own scars lining his body that it was there. It was like she wanted to meet him but at the same time wanted nothing more than for him to leave. Halfway between fight and flight. It intrigued and perturbed Julian all at once.

And that third thing he knew about the golden-haired stranger making her way toward him?

She was beautiful.

Long braids thrown over each shoulder shone in the Tennessee sun and complemented a complexion formed by a life out in the elements instead of tucked in front of electronic screens. Crystal-blue irises took him in as his gaze dropped to the freckles dusting her cheeks. Those freckles, he had no doubt, probably made several other appearances across the skin of her arms and legs as well, but for now were hidden beneath a long-sleeved dress and a pair of black tights. It was a modest outfit, yet Julian didn't miss the pleasant curves beneath the clinging fabric. She wore flats but only had to tilt her head up a fraction to see into his eyes as she came to a stop in front of him.

"Well, you sure are punctual, aren't you, Mr. Mercer?" She held out her hand.

He shook it. "Is that a problem?"

"Absolutely not." Her polite smile stayed just as polite. "It's just not that common around here. Most guests end up stopping along the road to take pictures. One time a couple showed up an hour late because they spotted a black bear hanging out in a tree." She glanced down at her watch. It was one of those smart watches made for exercise. The time popped up on the screen as she moved her wrist slightly. "You said you were going to be here at eleven on the dot and here you are."

"You can thank my military training for that," he said with a wry smile. "I don't think I could be late for something if I wanted to."

She laughed. Julian made sure not to trace the scar against her cheek with his eyes again.

"Well, either way, I'm happy you made it." She angled her body and spread her arms wide toward the house. "I'm Madeline Nash, and this is the Hidden Hills Inn."

The bed-and-breakfast was aptly named. Near the heart of the very small town of Overlook, Tennessee, the road to the inn wound its way through fields, forests and hills. Mountains crested in the distance. No sound of cars or city life broke through them or the land they were boxing in. Julian had gone from big-city Tennessee to small-town Tennessee to this rural beauty. The inn was in the center of it all yet felt a world away from everything else.

Julian appreciated the quiet, just as he did the privacy.

"Let's get you all signed in and then we can start the tour," Madeline continued. He followed her up to the long covered porch. She paused before opening the front door. "I'm sorry but it wasn't clear on the phone, are you expecting to meet someone here or are you traveling alone?"

"It's just me. I'm alone."

Madeline kept smiling. Customer service was in her wheelhouse and it showed. She kept to small talk without it ever feeling like small talk. After Julian signed in, she took him on a tour of the wide two-story house with all the best efforts of a seasoned host. From the common rooms to the private suites to the small bar that made up the surprisingly comfortable lounge at the back of the house, Madeline Nash made every space interesting and somehow intimate.

When the tour concluded at the bottom of one of the two sets of stairs the house offered, his golden-haired tour guide fixed him with a grin.

"I'll leave you to it," she said, already taking a step back. "If you need anything, don't hesitate to call the number on the card in your room. Breakfast and dinner are served every morning and night at seven. There's a list of activities and sights you might consider during your stay in a packet on your bed."

Julian had a flash of impulsive bravado. He almost asked the innkeeper if she ever considered accompanying guests to those sights and activities when a car door slammed outside. They both turned to the entryway window. A man with dark hair and a cowboy hat started up the walkway.

Madeline didn't say it out loud but she wasn't happy to see him. Her already-tense body tightened. Yet her smile stayed where it was.

"Again, if you have any questions, don't hesitate to ask."

Julian tipped his head in acknowledgment as Madeline left through the front door, greeting the man. Instead of coming inside, they moved across the yard and disappeared from view. A part of Julian wanted to follow, to make sure she was okay, but then his senses came back.

He didn't know Madeline and thinking he had to protect her was foolish. His mother would have scolded him for his presumptions that the innkeeper was some kind of hurt, damaged woman in need of saving. For cripes' sake, he'd only just met her.

Julian knew from experience that there were more people walking the earth with scars than with smooth, untouched skin. That didn't mean he had to try to save them all.

That didn't mean they needed saving in the first place.

First impressions were tricky like that.

The first smile was easy.

It was everything after that got a little murky when trying to decipher them.

His room was in the far corner of the second-floor landing. It was a big difference from the hotel rooms he'd been frequenting and, if he was being honest, the apartment he'd been living in the last several years. The room was spacious and stretched much wider than he thought was possible. Not only was there a king-size bed, there was an adjoining sitting area and a desk and a three-piece bathroom. He was surprised and happy to note that the showerhead was high enough to allow him to stand up straight beneath it, a luxury his apartment had never afforded him. In his Special Forces unit he'd been known as the Lumberjack. It wasn't that inventive of a nickname but it was apt. Julian was built tall, wide and muscled like his father before him. Most times it translated into unintentional intimidation. Other times it meant he had to hunch over in the shower.

Julian threw his bag down just as his phone started to ring.

The caller ID read Chance Montgomery.

"Mercer," Julian greeted. He walked to one of the windows that ran along the room and looked through the blinds. He spotted Madeline at the table where she'd been sitting when he'd pulled up earlier. Her male companion stood across from her. Julian couldn't get a read off of him.

"You know, we've been friends for a few years now," Chance said in his Southern twang. "Answering with a 'hello' or even a 'howdy' instead of your last name would make our conversations a little more casual and a little less like I've just accidentally called my old high school math teacher and she's still mad about the gum I put on her chair that one time."

Julian chuckled.

"Old habits die hard," he responded, actively loosening his shoulders by rolling them. "Brevity and precision have been my friends in the military for a while now."

"Luckily for you, the private sector has a lot fewer friends." He paused and then laughed. "Well, you know what I mean."

"It means I need to say 'howdy' apparently."

Chance laughed again.

"You can't see it but I'm giving you a type of salute you also wouldn't find in the military. It has to do something with a certain finger."

They joked around for a few more minutes before Chance finally circled back to the reason for the call. Julian didn't mind the chatter; in fact, it was one of the reasons he was headed to Chance's workplace in Alabama. Chance, a cowboy by upbringing but, lately, a surprisingly skilled bodyguard, was one of the few civilian friends Julian had kept through his marine service over the last ten years. Julian not only liked him but was confident he could work alongside him, which was why he was interviewing at the private protection firm Chance's uncle owned.

"I just wanted to make sure you were stopping to smell the roses in Overlook and not rushing here," Chance said, losing his earlier humor. "The interview isn't until next week and as long as I've known you, you haven't had a vacation, one that actually counted. So I'll reiterate one more time and then let it go. Enjoy yourself, go watch a sunset, sleep in, buy a lady a drink. You'll thank me for that advice when you're out in Germany away from all the Southern hospitality you've been hitting on your way here."

Julian knew Chance was right. His last deployment before he officially left the military started the week after his interview. Then he would hopefully return to Alabama and finally, finally stay put for a while.

"I'll make sure to smell the roses," Julian promised. "I'm here for two days and then on to Nashville for the next three. I should be at your place after that."

Chance must have thought this was acceptable. He ended the call without any more constructive criticism. Julian stayed at his spot by the window, admiring the curve of the mountain in the distance. Then his gaze dropped to the innkeeper.

Two days here and then he'd be one step closer to a new life.

"I'M NOT TRYING to destroy the family, Des."

Madeline Nash watched as her brother tried to save face moments after showing his backside. He took his dark gray Stetson, pressed it against his thigh and blew out a sigh she recognized as frustration.

"I didn't say that and you know it."

Madi pulled out her long braids, tamed the waves with her fingers and then sectioned her hair again. She separated it into three parts. Ever since she was a little girl she did what her eldest brother, Declan, had dubbed "angry-braiding." It wasn't like she could correct him. The evidence throughout her thirty years of life was fairly damning. Every scowl or frown captured in photographs or home movies was accompanied by long braids down her back or across her shoulders.

Some people counted to ten to cool off; she made her hair more manageable.

"You didn't have to say the words, Des. You gave me that look and then that tone. Don't for a minute deny it, either. Even outside our triplet telepathy I know your moods."

Desmond rolled his eyes. It was his trademark move for their disagreements.

"All I asked was if you had been to the ranch lately," Des countered. "I didn't suggest you were destroying anything, let alone our family."

Madi tried not to let the guilt move into her gut

again. Instead she channeled her irritation. Her hands went across her chest and her chin rose a fraction.

"And why would you ask that? You've never asked about me going to the ranch before."

"Because up until three months ago, you lived on that ranch."

If Desmond had been anyone else, Madi would have blushed at how childish she knew she sounded. But he was her brother. So she huffed and pretended there was nothing wrong with what she'd just said. She finished the braid over her left shoulder, then looked at anything but him.

"For your information, I had lunch with Ma and Nina a few weeks ago and it was lovely."

Desmond gave her a pointed stare.

"And was that at the ranch or in town?"

It was Madi's turn to roll her eyes. It didn't matter that she was an adult who had opened and currently ran her own business; Desmond still found a way to make her feel like she was a child again. A child who was perpetually in need of a guide to help her through the life he thought she should be living. It was at all times frustrating; seldom was it touching. In those few instances, a voice deep inside Madi would remind her why Desmond was protective of her more than he was with her brothers.

Now wasn't that time.

"You're making it sound like I've abandoned my family," she said. "As you said yourself, I've lived on that ranch for basically all of my life. I don't have to set foot on the property every day, you know."

Des rolled his eyes again. They were bright and ever-changing blue, just like hers and Caleb's. Madi felt another jab of guilt looking into them. He'd been the first person she'd told about her dream of running a bed-and-breakfast and the first person who had encouraged her to follow that dream when the old Richman house had gone up for sale.

Even now, after her childishness, he kept to the high road.

"I'm not saying you are obligated to check in. You don't have to go to the ranch at all, but you need to at least own up to the reason why you're currently not making any appearances there." His expression softened. "You're avoiding Mom and you know it."

Madi did know it but she didn't dare admit it. Thankfully, she didn't have to find a way to avoid the truth he was pointing out to her a moment longer. Like she knew his moods, she had to concede that he knew hers. Des took his cue to leave with grace. He walked around the table, gave her a kiss on the forehead and smiled. Then on went the Stetson.

"I really am proud of what you've done here, Madi. So are Mom and the others. Give them a chance to prove it to you."

Madi watched him leave without another word.

In the small town of Overlook, Tennessee, there were no hotels or motels. If you wanted a place to lay your head, then you'd have to leave town limits to get it. The Hidden Hills Inn was Overlook's quick and easy option for tourists who'd rather not bust their budgets by trying to rent one of the few cabins deeper in the forest and near the mountains. Or at the Wild Iris Retreat.

There was that flare of guilt again.

Her family owned the retreat. One Madi had left to open her own version of a hotel.

They're different, she reminded herself. The retreat was for guests seeking an authentic experience of living on a ranch and staying on the land. Hidden Hills was just a cozy, less expensive place to spend a night or two. *I'm not stealing anyone from Mom! They have more business than I do!*

Someone cleared their throat behind her. Madi jumped clear out of her seat.

"Whoa there!" Julian had his hands out as if he could steady her despite the distance between them. "Sorry! I thought you heard me."

Madi put her palm against her chest and gave him an embarrassed smile.

"No worries. I was just stuck in my own head." She motioned to the road that Des had just driven away on. "My brother has a habit of making me think too hard."

Julian took the joke with a good laugh and what almost looked like a dose of relief. Though maybe that was a touch of wishful thinking on Madi's part. There was no denying Julian Mercer was a handsome man. His hair was as black as night and cropped close, neat. His eyes were dark, too, but held a softness to them as they moved to hers. While he was a tall, obviously muscled man, the sharp angles of his nose and jaw were an elegant kind of ruggedness. Madi placed his age around her own and noted on reflex that his ring finger was very much bare.

"Family has a funny way of doing that, don't they?"

Madi nodded. Heat surprised her by moving up to her cheeks beneath the man's dark gaze. It inspired an offer she didn't have time to think about before saying.

"Would you like to join me, Mr. Mercer?" She waved to the table behind her; the lemonade pitcher on its surface had more than enough for two more glasses left in it. "Unless you would prefer to be alone, which is absolutely fine."

The man's smile only stretched.

"You can call me Julian," he said, moving around her to the other chair. Its dainty size made him look even more rugged and muscled. Still, there was a softness to his eyes. One that, despite herself, intrigued Madi.

"And you can call me Madi. Madeline was my grandmother."

Julian nodded and watched politely as she flipped a cup right side up from the serving tray and filled it. He chuckled before taking a drink.

"What's so funny?"

"My friend just told me I need to learn how to enjoy myself more. One thing he suggested?" He tipped his glass toward her. "Buy a lady a drink. I was wondering if this counts?"

The heat in her face started to travel south, propelled by the glint in his eye. Madi knew it was probably just her imagination and yet…

"I wouldn't say that it doesn't."

Julian's eyebrow arched but his smile stayed.

"I can work with that."

They lapsed into a pleasant conversation. It stretched into a walk along one of the trails. Then that became dinner. A proper drink came after.

Madi was too wrapped up in the unexpected great time to notice that the figure out in the woods that night wasn't just a shadow between the trees. It was a man.

Watching.

Waiting.

Chapter Two

Six months later, Madi was standing on the back porch, trying really hard to convince herself that she wasn't thinking about Julian Mercer. There wasn't time, and even if there were, she had already gone down that particular road so much that her tires were absolutely bare. Her metaphorical tires. Her real tires were in fine condition and attached to the van she hadn't wanted, but needed, to buy.

She replaced the mental image of smiling Julian Mercer with one of her behind the wheel, gunning in the direction of Loraine Wilson. She knew it wasn't polite, but it made her smile to imagine wiping the smug look off that wealthy woman's face.

Madi knew a murderous rampage was taking her irritation too far, but she could blame it on her hormones.

Being pregnant, in the Tennessee summer heat

no less, had stretched her patience and politeness thin.

"How are you doing it?"

Jenna Diggins—Hidden Hills' chef, bartender and occasional cleaner—nodded toward the stone pathway that led from the backyard and forked between the rental cabin and a small nature trail. Loraine, one of three guests currently booked at Hidden Hills, was pacing across it, immersed in her phone conversation.

"How am I doing what?" Madi asked, feigning innocence. Jenna wasn't just the only other employee—she had been Madi's friend for a decade.

Jenna giggled. She bumped her shoulder against Madi's.

"How are you destroying Mrs. Pearls and Coiffed Hair?"

Madi swatted at the woman but didn't deny anything.

"*Destroying* seems like such a harsh word. What I'm doing is simply giving her a love bump with my new mom van." She paused, then grinned. "Over and over again."

Jenna laughed and handed her a bottle of water from her backpack. Madi took it, grateful.

Summer in Tennessee was just about Madi's favorite time. Every tree and flower was teeming with life; every stream, creek and river was asking for companionship; and the skies stayed a shade

of blue that had a way of making Madi appreciate life all the way down in her bones.

Or at least that had been her feeling about the
sunny season before she'd been pregnant.

Now the sun made her already-hot body hotter,
the trees and flowers stood by as the mosquitoes
and bugs dive-bombed her every chance they got,
and the blue of the sky was a reminder that she
wasn't the same woman she had been the year before. Just like she wouldn't be the same woman
next year, either.

The water was the only part of summer that
Madi remained fond of, which was why she was
getting ready to show the guests to the creek in
the nearby forest that stretched across the property
line. Madi had grown up taking advantage of the
creeks and ponds and rivers to cool off. Not even
Loraine's passive-aggressive comments could de-
rail her plans to enjoy herself today.

Someone cleared their throat behind them. Heat
instantly flooded Madi's cheeks. Ray Cutler, the
guest staying in the rental cabin, gave them a hu-
moring look.

"Don't worry," he said. "After listening to her
go on and on about how she had to let her dog
nanny go because she was positive he was watching her Netflix, I can appreciate your frustration."

Jenna laughed but Madi still felt shame at being
caught bad-mouthing a guest. After her whirl-

wind romance earlier that year she'd made a vow to never stray into unprofessional territory again. She should have known better. Yet there she was prattling on about how she'd like to run over someone less than two yards away.

"It's the hormones making me cranky," she said, knowing it was a lame excuse. "That and the heat, and I can't stop babbling nonsense." Jenna snorted. Madi pushed on. "Are you ready to go, Ray?"

Ray was what Madi's mother, Dorothy, would call a middle man. He wasn't short but he wasn't tall. There was no myriad of muscles filling out his clothes but he wasn't bone thin, either. He had one of those faces that seemed to be universally familiar, pleasant to look at but not knee-buckling handsome. His hair was a dirty blond, cut short and wavy, and for the last two days he'd been sporting a pair of glasses across his dark eyes. His personality so far had fallen in the middle, too. Polite and quiet but vocal when you hit the right topic. Madi liked the man because—unlike Loraine and her husband, Nathan—his love for the outdoors and Overlook seemed genuine. He cracked a broad smile.

"Two lovely ladies taking little ole me out to the creek on a hot summer day? This day would only get better if I could go back and tell my fifth-grade self about it."

Madi and Jenna laughed and soon they were off across the stone path. Loraine ended her call but didn't seem interested in focusing on her husband. Instead she breezed past him and matched Madi's pace when the stones ended and the dirt trail began.

"Sorry about that," she started, waving her smartphone around. "You'd think our gardener would know what we want by now. Do I like succulents? Yes. Do I want them in my bedroom? No. Roses are the only flower I'll allow in there, and only on special occasions. You'd think after working for us for over a year he'd know better." She let out a long, dramatic sigh. "But I suppose it isn't his fault. His daughter is trying to become some kind of interior designer. She's been trying to use me for practice. Stick with what you know, little girl. I'm not running some kind of weird work charity."

Loraine gave Madi a look that clearly said she was waiting to be agreed with. Madi begrudgingly flexed her customer service muscles.

"Working relationships are hard to navigate sometimes. I used to work with my family before I opened Hidden Hills. It definitely can be tricky."

Loraine nodded emphatically. Her hair, a teased-out red that matched her shade of lipstick and her purse, barely moved at the motion. A look of disgust flitted across her impeccably made-up face.

"My Nathan is a wonderful man in the board-room but I barely can stand him at the house sometimes. I can't imagine working alongside him, either. He's been talking about retiring early and staying at home and that just makes my skin crawl." Loraine let out a laugh. It wasn't a good one. From Madi's experience with the socialite during the past two days, she knew what was coming next. "Maybe I should do what you did. Buy a funny little house out in the middle of nowhere to keep myself busy. How fun would that be?"

Madi couldn't blame the pregnancy hormones on the rage that kicked up in her chest. Luckily, she didn't have the time to regret anything she might have said. Loraine prattled on without a care in the world.

And right onto the worst subject she could have prattled about.

"Though I suppose you won't be doing this for much longer. Once that baby of yours is here you won't have time to be a single mother and run your little inn." Madi must have made a face. Loraine adopted a look of concern. Madi doubted it was real. "Oh, honey, just remember, there's no shame in raising a kid all on your own. Whoever the father is, I'm sure you had nothing to do with him abandoning you. Try not to beat yourself up about it, okay? It isn't healthy for you or the baby."

Every part of Madi tensed. Her shoulders, her jaw, her fists. Her heart. Good customer service and good manners became just words in her head. Loraine Wilson continued to smile. There was a pointedness to it. An edge. Sharper than she'd expect from the wife of a rich businessman from Portland.

Loraine was intentionally trying to rile her up. Why?

Was she that bored? Was she that unhappy in her own life that she had to tear down others?

"Hey, Madi! Could I steal you for a second? I have a question about tonight's dinner."

Bless her heart, Jenna appeared at Madi's other elbow like a guardian angel. She gave her a squeeze that brought Madi out of her angry haze and back to reality.

"Sure, let's talk." Madi pointed a small nod and an even smaller smile at Loraine. "Just keep following the path. If you'll excuse me a moment." The woman seemed put out that the conversation was ending and let her husband, Nathan, who had been trailing behind them deep in his business call, walk alongside her.

Madi and Jenna waited until there were a few feet between them and started walking again.

"That was uncalled-for," Jenna said in a harsh whisper. "Want me to go get the van?"

Madi didn't mean what she said next but her heart was hurting. And she was sure that Loraine had done that on purpose.

"Forget the van. I'd like results faster than that."

Jenna's expression softened. She put her arm around her friend. They walked the rest of the way to the creek without saying a word.

The pain in Madi's chest only grew once she dipped her feet into the cool, crisp water.

Madi felt no joy in it.

And that was Loraine's fault, too.

THE DAY CRAWLED into night. After showing the guests the creek, Madi busied herself with chores around the inn. For the first time since opening Hidden Hills, she skipped dinner with the guests. Not that it was required of her or even asked, yet she had thought it was a nice touch. Tonight she couldn't stomach sitting there and pretending everything was all right.

It wasn't.

Even before Loraine showed up.

It had been almost five months since Madi had found out she was pregnant. In that time a lot of things had gone right and wrong. The inn had hit its stride for a few months and made Madi money rather than just breaking even. She threw herself into work and welcomed the distraction that kept her thoughts away from the fact that Julian Mercer was nowhere to be found.

The number he'd given her was disconnected. The emails she'd sent bounced back. His social media existed but wasn't active. They'd spent two amazing, surprising and magical days together that had turned into a week. One blissful week she had never imagined would be as great as it had been. Yet the moment Julian's SUV had disappeared down the road on his way out, it was like the man had vanished completely.

Since then the burn of anger and embarrassment had cooled. The drive to be the best parent she could be had taken its place. Along with what she had thought was acceptance. Never seeing the father of her unborn child again was a harsh reality, sure, but what had she really expected? What they'd had was, to her, once-in-a-lifetime hot, but once in a lifetime nonetheless. Julian had been a ship passing in the night. A momentary escape.

Though that had been her decision, hadn't it?

Could she be mad at him for being radio silent after she'd been the one who said their week together was all they should have?

Madi ran her hand over her naked belly. The water from the bath had never been that warm. Now it was cold. She was only fooling herself. Almost every single time she felt her stomach she thought about Julian. Where was the mountain of a man who had rocked her world? She felt an emptiness that let Madi know she hadn't accepted anything. At least, not with any enthusiasm.

The music that had been playing from her phone lowered. A rhythmic sequence of beeps filled the bathroom as a call came through. Jenna's name scrolled along the screen. Madi wasn't about to ignore her friend, even if she'd asked not to be disturbed.

Madi sloshed water out of the tub and with wet fingers answered the phone.

"Hello?"

"Sorry to mess up your quiet night," Jenna said, diving in. "But, uh, I have Nathan here with me right now and—" There was a rustling sound as she must have moved away from the man. She lowered her voice as she continued. "He wants to know if you and Loraine are done talking."

Madi gave her reflection in the mirror over the sink a dubious look before grabbing her towel to dry off.

"Come again?"

"Right? That's what I was thinking when he asked but he said that you called Loraine an hour ago and asked her to come up to your room. He tried calling her to come to dinner but the phone went straight to voice mail. He didn't want to come up there because he didn't know the rules."

Madi felt her eyebrows fly high.

"Why would I do any of that? I wanted to not be disturbed because of Loraine. She was two seconds out from getting popped in the face."

"Nathan seems adamant."

Madi sighed.

"Tell him to go ahead and call Loraine again. She was probably just tying up the phone line with her gardener complaining about life."

Jenna repeated the suggestion while Madi bent down awkwardly. She felt around for the drain plug and shouldered the phone. When a song started blaring from the next room she nearly dropped both.

"What in the world?"

"What?" Jenna asked, voice still low.

Madi pulled the drain plug up and placed it on the counter. She shook her hand off and looked at the door separating her from the small living area. A weird knot started to tighten in Madi's stomach. She slipped into her robe.

"What's going on, Madi?"

"I think Loraine might really be in my living room," she whispered. "A phone is going off."

Jenna said something, but for the life of her, Madi couldn't pay attention to what it was. Her focus narrowed to pinpoint precision. She opened the door, ready to confront the woman who was still managing to ruin her day, but found it empty. Or, at least, no one was around.

A cell phone continued to play music from the coffee table. It wasn't the only thing out of place. A shotgun sat next to it. Madi's blood ran cold.

"That's Dad's."

"What's going on, Madi?"

Madi felt like she was falling down some wild rabbit hole. She knew that shotgun. Her father's initials were carved into the grip. Right next to her grandfather's. It was supposed to be at the ranch.

Not on her coffee table with a phone that wasn't hers.

The phone finally stopped ringing. Madi touched the gun, running her finger over her dad's initials to make sure it was real.

"I'm coming up," Jenna said, no longer trying to be discreet.

Madi heard the concern, knew she should say something, but another detail caught her attention.

Her bedroom door was closed.

With steps that felt like wading through water, Madi went to the door and swung it wide.

"Oh my God."

She saw the pearls around the woman's neck first. The dark red, tight-fitted dress second. The Louboutin pumps third.

Finally, as though her eyes had been reluctant,

Madi saw the woman's red hair. It flowed around a disfigured face covered in blood.

She was dead.

And if Madi were a betting woman, she'd wager that the gun lying on her coffee table had been used to murder Loraine Wilson.

Chapter Three

"And you think *this* is a good idea?"

Chance Montgomery gave him a look filled with skepticism.

"I never said it was a *good* idea," Julian admitted. "I just said it *was* an idea."

They were standing on the side of the road, their cars parked in front of the town of Overlook welcome sign. It was as quaint as Julian remembered. Worn but filled with charm. Two small spotlights lit up the hand-painted letters. It sent a warm glow bouncing off the hood of his truck.

It probably would have been better to come back during the day but the pull of seeing the Overlook innkeeper had tugged Julian right off the road to his new life.

Chance took his cowboy hat off. He'd been finishing up a personal matter in North Tennessee and had met up with Julian to caravan on the way back to Alabama. He sucked on the toothpick between his lips. He'd gotten it from the diner where they'd eaten an hour ago. In another hour they were supposed to be stopping at a hotel. The next day, Tuesday, they'd be in Alabama at the security firm. Next Monday would be Julian's first official day as a private bodyguard.

His first official day in his new life.

Yet there they were.

"Well, I can't really tell you not to do it," Chance said. "Just that you might want to think it over a little. I can't say my track record with women has been outstanding but even I'd be a bit worried about rolling into town unannounced. You haven't talked since you left. That's a lot of time between then and now. A lot could have changed."

Julian knew better than anyone how different life could be from one moment to the next. He knew how just one second could irrevocably change everything. He also knew that dropping in after all this time could be construed as too much.

"Listen, I'm not going to go there and stand outside in the rain with a stereo over my head and hearts in my eyes," Julian deadpanned. "I'm just going to see if there's an opening at the inn for the night and, if there is, see if she wants to grab a quick meal to catch up. Last we talked she was worried about the inn doing well and I was on the way to a job interview." He shrugged. "Nothing more or less than a conversation or two. Then I'm back on the road tomorrow. No harm, no foul."

"And if she doesn't want you there?"

Julian shrugged again, though he had to admit he didn't like the thought.

"Then I'm back on the road tonight."

Chance nodded, conceding to the logic. Plus, he was right, there wasn't much he could do to stop Julian from taking the detour.

"Well, here's to hoping she's not married and keeping your time together a secret from her husband," Chance teased. He clapped Julian on the shoulder and went back to his truck. Before he got in he paused and grinned. "And if she's happy to see you, well, then I guess I'll see you Monday morning."

Julian watched his friend take off down the road before he got back into his own truck. There he sat and stared at the sign for a moment. It had been over half a year since Julian had seen Madi Nash. For all he knew she *could* absolutely be married. She could have sold the inn. She could have moved.

She could be happy to see him.

She could wish he hadn't shown up at all.

Julian scrubbed a hand down his face and exhaled. He'd been deployed six times in his career, three of those in combat zones. He'd set boots down in the dusty heat of Iraq. He'd navigated the islands of Japan with little more than a partially busted radio. He'd even, to the chagrin of their

spec-ops commander, fought his way through a
bar brawl in Germany. And yet here he was, in
small-town Tennessee, actually nervous that a
golden-haired, freckled-skinned bed-and-breakfast owner was going to put him in his place.

How the mighty had fallen.

Not that he'd counted himself as mighty.

Julian finally turned the engine over and got
back onto the road. He marveled at the fact that
he remembered the town as well as he did. The
streetlamps across the main strip cast light on
the same businesses he remembered, just as the
moonlight shone across the houses and landscapes
he'd passed before. Not much had changed. He
knew plenty of people, including those he'd served
with, who would have been bored by the lack of
change. Julian welcomed the familiarity. It was
everything he was hoping to have for himself
when he finally got settled in his new job. Roots.
Ones that grounded him. Ones that centered him.

A life that would start after the detour.

The GPS on his phone remained off as the
houses turned to fields, the fields turned to trees,
and the trees started to open up to the inn's property, which he'd recalled countless times in the
last half year. Despite all of his resolve, he was
starting to feel something like nerves when the
drive curved, indicating the inn was almost in
sight. In his mind Julian had already pulled into

one of the spots, gotten out of the car with calmness and determination and bounded up the stairs with a smile on his face.

However, what really happened when the road straightened and the inn came into view was drastically different.

Blue and red lights were strobing from the tops of two parked deputy cruisers. One had two uniforms standing next to it. They were talking to a man Julian recognized from pictures in Madi's room as one of her triplet brothers. A truck was pulled up on the grass next to him, and in the far corner of the lot was something that made Julian even more uneasy.

It was a coroner's van.

Julian coasted to a stop far enough away from the closest cruiser so everyone could still drive around him. By the time he cut his engine, one of the deputies was on his way over. The other seemed to be in deep conversation with Desmond Nash. Neither of them looked his way.

"Howdy there," the deputy greeted. His voice was tight. As was his body language. "How can I help you?"

Julian wished he were a people person, but he knew better. Sure, he prided himself on being a good friend, but putting strangers at ease had never been in his wheelhouse. He didn't have the patience, especially now.

"I'm here about a room," he stated without any preamble. "What's going on?"

The deputy looked like a man who very much did not like what was going on. His jaw hardened.

"There's been an incident that we're investigating." He cast a look back at the inn. Jenna, Madi's friend and employee, shut the front door behind her with enough vigor to draw the attention of everyone outside. She didn't look sorry for the force. Though when she swept her gaze across her onlookers as she stepped off the porch, she stopped with obvious surprise at Julian.

Neither had a chance to explain.

The door behind Jenna opened. A dark-skinned woman with a badge swinging against her chest came out. Her face was impassive, frown set so deep that Julian tensed even more than he thought was possible.

That was when he saw Madi.

In the distance between them the glow of moonlight mixed with the whirls of blue and red. It was unsettling.

But what put fire in Julian's gut the most?

Madi's hands were handcuffed in front of her.

A uniform led her out, hand against her back. Her eyes stayed on the porch as she walked to the steps.

"What's going on?" Julian asked, his voice becoming an octave too low. The deputy tensed in return. His hand moved near the butt of his service weapon. Julian made sure not to move another inch, but couldn't stop himself from yelling when she was waiting for her escort to open the back of the closest cruiser. "Madi?"

For a moment Julian was worried she hadn't heard him. But then she turned, first her face and then her entire body. From the side Julian noticed something he hadn't seen when she'd first walked through the front door.

Her stomach.

Her *pregnant* stomach.

Part of Julian's mind went into overdrive; the other, cool-under-pressure part gave him the patience to stay still.

Madi's eyes widened in surprise, just as Jenna's had.

"I didn't do it," she yelled. "I swear!"

Then, in a movement that was neither harsh nor easy to watch, Madi was ushered into the back seat. When the door closed behind her, all Julian could do was stare.

GRANDMA MADELINE NASH had always said a person was never given more than they could handle in life. She'd said it when their house was destroyed in a flood, when the ranch fell on hard times, after her husband passed away, when the triplets were abducted and right through the aftermath of the attack, leading up to her only son's death.

Madi put her head in her hands. She had a hard time believing she could handle everything like her namesake had. She'd been at the Wildman County Sheriff's Department for almost five hours. In that time she'd been handcuffed to a metal table in the interrogation room before being uncuffed and brought a rolling office chair because it had more padding. During those five hours she'd only spoken to three people.

The first had been Detective Santiago, her brother's partner. Jazz was a family friend but treated Madi with short, clipped questions. Where had Madi been in the hours leading up to dinner? Why had she called Loraine? If she hadn't done it, then why did the call log on her phone say she had? Where did she get the shotgun?

How badly had she hated the woman?

Madi had gone over her afternoon and night several times before Jazz excused herself. Her brother Caleb never came in.

Declan, the sheriff and Madi's eldest brother, eventually did and explained why.

"Caleb can't work this case because he can't get his emotions in check," Declan had said. He hadn't sat down across from her. His body was riddled with tension, his face pulled down in a frown. Madi didn't need any triplet connection to know he was trying his best to keep his own emotions in check. "Him working this case is a big-time conflict of interest. Jazz will take over as well as a detective from the local PD in Kilwin down the road."

"She's teaming up with the police department?" Madi had been stunned at the news. The two only ever worked together on emergencies like high-speed chases that crossed the town limits or manhunts that spanned the county. Now they were doing the same with her?

It made her already-knotted stomach quake.

Declan had sighed.

"It was at Mayor Harding's suggestion, and honestly, it took all I had to convince him to keep us on the case. You have two brothers on the force. Our family history doesn't help. This is only going to rock the boat on public perception of us."

"Family history? Do you mean the abduction?" she had nearly shrieked. "We were eight! How is that our fault?"

"I'm not blaming any of you for that, and you know that. I meant what happened with Caleb last year. I think the mayor would like the Nashes out of the spotlight for a while. Even though you know as well as I do that the town has never really let go of what happened when you were kids."

Madi did know that Overlook was incapable of forgetting one of its biggest unsolved mysteries. It wasn't every day that three children were attacked, abducted and held for three days before escaping on their own…and that, to this day, no one had ever been able to ID the man responsible. Never mind understanding his motive.

As far as what had happened with Caleb, talk had gotten out of hand quickly but had died down.

Or so Madi had thought.

"The mayor thinks it's best for you, the department and the town if we're extra careful with how we move forward," he continued, as if his words were scripted.

"And that means what exactly?"

Declan let out another long sigh. This time Madi saw the defeat in it.

"That means that my chief deputy will run point on this case while I handle the rest of the department and try to keep this in-house as much as I can. Past that, Caleb and I will have nothing to do with this case. We can't afford anyone blaming us for favoritism or being impartial."

Madi felt the tears spring to her eyes before they ever fell down her cheeks. She was angry. She was scared. Caleb being taken off the case made sense. Declan stepping away hadn't crossed her mind as a possibility.

Pain twisted his expression. His face softened.

"I know you didn't do it, Madi," he said, voice low. "But the evidence against you is pretty damning. I can't dismiss it, even though I know you're innocent. Hell, I think everyone in this department knows it, too. We just have to do our jobs and do them carefully, or we could end up hurting your cause instead of helping it." He reached out and touched her hand. "Jazz is great at her job. So are the rest of my people."

Madi wiped at her cheeks. She nodded.

"I understand."

He smiled but then let go of her hand. Then his face went stony.

"Are you sure there's no one who could corroborate your side of the story, though?"

Madi shook her head. She brought her hand down to her stomach.

"It was only the two of us."

Declan left soon after. Another hour went by. Madi's thoughts went between everything that had happened and the other surprise she'd gotten that night.

Julian Mercer.

In the flesh.

This might be too much for me to handle, Grandma, she thought ruefully.

The third person to visit her finally was Caleb. He moved into the room like they were teens again and sneaking out of the house to go to the barn loft to meet their friends. He hurried to her side and crouched down next to her. There was an undeniable excitement in his movements that she didn't understand.

"Why did you lie to us, Madi?" he asked in a rush. "Pride be damned, you're looking at murder charges!"

Madi felt her eyes widen. Did Caleb really think she killed Loraine?

"What are you—"

"You should have told us about your alibi the moment we showed up on scene!" Madi didn't know what he was talking about. She said as much. Caleb looked exasperated. "I know you didn't want to get him in trouble with his boss, but my God, Madi, this is serious."

"His boss?"

"Julian Mercer. Your alibi." He thumbed back to the door. "He just wrote his official statement about you two being together. I mean, yeah, I have some personal questions I'd like to ask—for instance, who the heck is this guy—but right now he could be that creep you dated in college and I'd be happy as punch."

Madi didn't have time to correct her brother before the door opened and in walked Declan and a man who must have been the lawyer.

They expressed the same sentiment.

Madi should have come clean about being with Julian during the afternoon and leading up to the discovery of Loraine's body, instead of trying to cover for him so he didn't get into any trouble with his boss. No one's job was worth the risk of her being suspected of murder.

Now they couldn't charge her. Which meant they couldn't hold her there any longer.

The air in the interrogation room became lighter. Her brothers' shoulders were no longer sagging. There was new life behind every word and movement. The entire mood had changed.

It made Madi realize how dire her situation had been before Julian's lie.

And that was what it was—a lie.

Yet with one hand resting on her pregnant belly, Madi realized it was a lie she wouldn't correct.

Not until Loraine's real murderer was caught.

Chapter Four

"So I've been downgraded to lead suspect instead of a shoo-in for murder."

Madi was as beautiful as Julian remembered but undoubtedly tired. Her eyes were red and swollen. She rubbed her hands together, fretting with nervous energy. They stood outside the Wildman County Sheriff's Department. A hint of the sunrise colored the distance. The air was cool and seemed to add to her discomfort.

Julian wanted to reach out and take all of the concern and worry away, but truth be told, he was out on his own limb of uncertainty.

He'd just lied to the authorities. In a big way, too.

"They're going to find the real person who did this," he said, hands shoved into his pockets to curb the urge to tuck a loose strand of her hair behind her ear. "Now that they aren't focused on you they can do that."

Madi shot a nervous look toward the front

doors. They were standing next to the sheriff's truck in the parking lot. Declan and Caleb were still inside. This time with the husband of the murdered woman. He'd been out-of-his-mind angry and had to be kept in a separate part of the building.

I don't care if she's pregnant! She killed my wife! She killed my Loraine! She needs to pay!

The man had been so certain of Madi's guilt, so incensed by it, that he had spit as he'd yelled. His fervor had solidified Julian's urge to help Madi.

He knew without a doubt that Madi was innocent. He'd felt it in his bones the moment she'd yelled out to him that she didn't do it. He'd jumped into his SUV and flown to the station, ready to watch as the rest of the department believed her, too.

Yet it didn't happen.

Or at least, the evidence forced their hands.

The looks across the local deputies' faces changed as the hours wore on. Julian stayed in the lobby with the flimsy reasoning of being a friend of Madi's. He waited to be questioned but no one ever came for him. In all the uproar he'd seemingly melted away into the scenery. He'd only had the chance to talk to Jenna to get the quick and short story of what had happened before she'd had to leave. The sheriff and Caleb could be seen, angry and whispering. The entire department's mood went from determined to find the alternate story to souring. Then on edge. When Julian had seen the lawyer come in through the lobby, wearing a suit and an expression that meant he was in for a rough ride, the need to help Madi had punched through Julian's gut until he was standing in front of her brother and lying through his teeth.

Now he was standing in front of Madi and telling the same lie.

"I sneaked in an hour before Jenna called you, parking my vehicle off the road and hiding in the trees so no one knew I was there. That's why you didn't want to eat dinner with the guests, which is unlike you," he spelled out. "I was with you in the bathroom when Jenna called. You found the body, but I was next to you. Realizing the cops were going to be involved, I went out the window and made it to my car. Then I pretended to come in for the first time so no one would suspect I'd been there at all."

Madi's eyes were wide and blue. Oh so blue.

"And the reason I didn't want to be caught up in an investigation was because I was worried that it would get me fired before I ever started my job next week." Julian shrugged. "Not a noble story, but everyone in there knows you didn't do it so it made sense to them."

The innkeeper ran a hand over her belly. Her

pregnant belly. Julian wanted to ask how far along she was but getting their story straight here, now, was the most important thing they could talk about. As she'd already said, it was a lie that had made the difference between murderer and lead suspect.

"Why?" she finally asked. "You... Well, you don't know me. This could absolutely get you fired *and* jail time." She lowered her voice and took a step closer. Julian could reach out and touch that baby bump between them if he were so inclined. "Why take that risk? Why lie?"

Julian gave her the honest truth.

"You said you didn't do it and I believe you."

A look he couldn't interpret crossed the innkeeper's expression. Then it transformed back into exhaustion.

"And am I to guess what we were doing together in secret last night?"

Julian felt the heat of their earlier intimate memories burn through him. Just as they had been throughout the last several months. Like lighter fluid thrown into a low flame. Hot, alarming and just a dangerous taste of what else could happen.

"The same thing we did last time I was here," he answered. "Apparently, Caleb had no idea you and I had been romantic then. I had to tell him otherwise to give credence to my story now."

Again, Julian wanted to search her expression

to find the reason why she'd ended things, why she'd kept him a secret then and the time after he'd left, but he had to focus. Not that he could have gleaned the truth from the woman standing so close to him. Her expression was as guarded as her brothers' had been when they'd brought her in. Maybe it was a Nash family trait.

"And why did you show up? Outside the fiction you've been spinning about our romantic encounter."

Julian tried to smile, tried to downplay the eagerness he'd hidden from Chance when he'd decided to visit Hidden Hills. This time he lowered his voice.

"I just wanted to say hi before I went on to my new life."

Madi was quick to comment. She wasn't smiling.

"And now you're my alibi in a murder investigation where I'm the lead suspect. If that's not good—or bad—timing, I don't know what is."

Silence stretched between them for a few moments. Madi looked down at her hands on her stomach. Her expression was knotted in thought. When she met his eyes again there was a fire behind them. However, before she could speak, the door to the department swung open.

Caleb took the stairs down two at a time. When

he got to them, he clapped Julian on the back and smiled for all he was worth.

"While I'm not exactly happy you waited so long to do it, I'm sure as hell glad you came forward," he said, reiterating what he'd told Julian earlier. He gave his sister an equally enthusiastic smile. "I'm just glad we can all go home now."

Madi didn't share in his exuberance.

"My home is a crime scene," she pointed out.

Caleb nodded, deflating slightly.

"Good thing that's not the only home you have here."

Madi looked like she wanted to say something else but Caleb wasn't having it. The earlier stress had lifted. Now he was reveling in the lightness. Julian had been there before. He became reacquainted with the feeling at the end of every deployment.

Caleb motioned to his truck and addressed Julian directly.

"Why don't you two follow me?" he said, already digging out his keys. "Mom and Nina have some beds made up and some breakfast going, depending on how you're feeling."

Julian's eyebrow rose high.

"And where exactly are we going?"

The detective gave them both a grand smile.

"The Nash Family Ranch! Where else?"

THE SUNLIGHT MET them and followed them across town and right up to and through the entrance to the Nash Family Ranch. The last time she'd talked to Julian, Madi had been avoiding the ranch and her mother out of guilt.

Things hadn't gotten much better. When she'd announced her pregnancy her mother had been happy, but also angry.

It had created a rift between them, one Madi's brothers had tried to repair, but they found no easy way to soften either woman. Because even though her situation wasn't ideal, Madi wouldn't allow any negativity. No matter if it was a passive-aggressive comment or a wayward glance that held an edge.

Now, though, as the fields passed by on either side of Julian's SUV and the ranch at the end of Winding Road became closer, Madi wanted to avoid her mother for an entirely new reason. Dorothy Nash had been through the wringer in the past three decades. She'd faced and dealt in heartache like she'd been cursed with bad luck. She'd seen needless violence and pain much more than any one person should have to bear.

And here Madi was, adding another heartache alongside the father of her child, who'd just committed a crime to keep her from being charged as a murderer.

Madi pressed her forehead against the cool of

the window. It sounded like the plot to a movie where Harrison Ford would eventually be jumping out of an airplane or from one skyscraper rooftop to another to save the day.

"So, *this* is the famous family ranch?"

Julian's eyes had been swiveling as he'd driven through the front gate that ended Winding Road. He was observant, that much Madi knew of the man. She had appreciated this skill during their week together. He'd noticed the shifts in her mood and thoughts with ease. He understood her.

Yet maybe that hadn't been something special between them. Maybe that was just who Julian was. An observant man who had come into town, flashed his smile and then disappeared.

Then again, she'd been the one who said leaving was okay.

So what that Julian hadn't reached out? He hadn't picked up a phone, hadn't sent an email, and the mailbox had remained free of any letter bearing his name.

That was what she had said she wanted, right?

Never to see him again?

Yet here he was.

It, along with everything else, filled Madi's head like rising water. There wasn't time to sort out what didn't make sense. All she could hope to do was survive it. To keep swimming. To escape the flood.

So she held her tongue back from asking why Julian had gone silent and why he was back. Instead, she tried to answer him like she would a guest. Forced jubilance and pride. Polite but not overly expressive. A good middle ground.

"Yes, this is it. The Nash Family Ranch. Home to several generations of Nashes throughout the many years it's been here." She motioned to a road that forked off the straightaway. "That leads to the Wild Iris Retreat, the stables, several trails and Caleb and Nina's new house." She hesitated before detailing the rest of the ranch's geography. The customer service lilt to her speech drained away. She couldn't hide the weight of what had happened pressing her next words down. "You know, I don't know if Mom has anyone staying at the retreat right now. If so, this could really hurt business. Maybe I shouldn't be here."

Julian shook his head. For a moment she thought he was going to reach out to her, but he kept his hands firmly on the steering wheel.

"I don't know your family but I have a feeling, just by what I've seen in the last few hours, that there's nowhere else they'd rather you be." This time his gaze swept over to her.

And then down to her stomach.

Madi ran her hand over it, as if she could shield herself from his questions. For months she had tried to tell him the very same thing she was trying not to bring up right now.

What if he reacted poorly? What if he decided to recant his statement? Madi now knew how bad things had looked for her with Loraine's murder. What if she was actually convicted?

She'd lose her daughter.

From there Madi's thoughts of the future spiraled. Fear and uncertainty pricked at her eyes, blurring her vision. She didn't realize they were at the main house until Julian cut the engine.

"Madi." His voice had gone low, a sound that normally put the fire of longing beneath her skin. This time, however, it wasn't the sound of lust she heard. It was severity. Like a moth to a flame, she met his stare. She was unable to look away as he continued. "There is nothing you can tell me that would make me take back the alibi. Okay?"

Madi shouldn't have been surprised that once again, Julian Mercer had read her like a book. He had a knack for that sort of thing. She nodded. He kept on.

"There's no ring on your finger. You're not married or engaged," he continued. "Are you seeing someone?"

"No."

Julian nodded, more to himself than the conversation.

Caleb's truck door slammed shut near them.

The porch light flipped on, bathing the SUV's cab in an eerie glow. Julian wasn't done yet, but Madi wanted to finish what she'd been trying to do for months.

Because as ridiculous as it was, Madi realized she trusted that Julian would keep his word. That even if he didn't like the news, he wouldn't betray her.

At least, she really hoped he wouldn't.

"Julian," she said, cutting him off just before he could say anything more, "she's yours."

Madi might have trusted the man, but in that moment, it was startlingly clear to her that she didn't have his gift of observation. She couldn't read his book. Not a single word.

Julian was a mystery to her.

And Madi was afraid he always would be.

Chapter Five

The low buzz from the air-conditioning was comforting. So was the softness of the sheets. The fabric softener's scent wrapped around Madi's senses like a warm embrace. She stretched her legs out and, for the briefest of moments, felt peace settle across her.

Then her bladder reminded her that not only had she just woken up, but she had just woken up pregnant.

She couldn't lounge in her bed.

And she wasn't in *her* bed.

That was when the insanity from the inn came back in full force. Madi groaned and struggled to sit up. The sheets might have been soft and smelled good, but they weren't hers. She was in the guest bedroom at Desmond's house. Through the open slats in the window she could see the roof of the main house in the distance. The house they'd all grown up in. The one their mother still lived in now.

Madi remembered how the Nash matriarch had looked at her when she and Julian stepped out of his SUV. Right after she'd told him the truth about the child she was carrying.

Right after neither had said a word once that truth had spread between them.

Dorothy Nash was an optimistic woman but Madi had seen the cracks in her armor in the light of dawn. No one in the Nash family was a stranger to how hard it could be to carry on. Still, her mother had worn her brave face with conviction as she'd embraced Madi. That affection had transferred to Julian, a man she'd never met, before ushering both inside for food.

Over that meal, Caleb had done most of the talking, laying out everything that had happened while Madi and Julian kept quiet. Madi knew she could tell her family anything without fear of being exposed as a liar but she didn't want to make *them* liars. So she ate her food and then accepted the room at Des's for a nap. Julian had been offered the other guest room, and she'd all but run to her bed before seeing if he had accepted it.

Madi felt for her phone on the nightstand before remembering she didn't have it. Her bladder's urgency became louder than the vulnerability she felt creeping in. She didn't stop to see who was or wasn't in the guest bedroom as she fled to the hall bathroom. It was only after she was finished and cleaned up that she paused at the closed door.

Hesitation wasn't just a word. It was a full-body experience for Madi, whose fist hovered next to the wood of the door. The twisted, horrible image of what had once been Loraine's face entered her mind.

If everything happened for a reason, Madi hated to know what the reason was.

Movement downstairs pulled Madi's attention. Her hesitation to talk to Julian turned into a resolution to avoid him for as long as she could. She hurried down the stairs, already pulling up a smile that sold the fact that she was okay.

That smile, fake or not, wavered when her mother bustled into view. Madi angry-braided. Her mother everything-braided. Today was no exception. She sported a tight silver braid over each shoulder and had her best pair of overalls on. She held up her late mother's outdoor serving platter, topped with several cups and a pitcher of tea.

"Hey, sweetie," she greeted, expression softening so much Madi could have used it as a pillow. "I was about to come up and wake you after I put this out." That soft expression started to harden. Madi followed her through the house, feeling the concern transfer.

"Why? What's going on?"

Her mother paused just before the front door. Her voice lowered.

"Caleb just showed up in a huff. I don't think any news he has is good." Madi fought the urge to gulp. Her mother leaned over to bump her shoulder. The ice cubes in the pitcher clinked against the glass. "But don't you worry, we're all going to get through this. We just need to band together and figure it all out."

Her mother flashed a reassuring smile and pushed through the door. Madi followed, hand already rubbing her stomach.

Between the main house and Desmond's was a small dirt path, a picnic table along with extra seating and a driveway that led to the main road that cut through the ranch. Their family was big on outdoor living. That always included eating and tea drinking. So a gathering at the table wasn't an unusual scene for the ranch. What *was* unusual was the company sitting at the table.

Julian stood as they got closer. Caleb was already on his feet, pacing the dirt beside the table with a phone against his ear. Neither man looked pleased.

"Hey."

Madi was ashamed at how Julian's baritone sang to her body, even in the most innocent of settings. She slid into the seat opposite him with a small "hey" of her own. He settled back in and smiled politely as her mother set a cup in front of him. His eyes remained grim.

"What's going on?" she asked, looking to her brother. He wasn't as tightly wound as he had been the night before but there was a definite weight there. Julian answered while Caleb finished up his call.

"Apparently after they let us go last night it was implied that the sheriff's department had already crossed the line and was playing favorites."

"That's ridiculous," her mother interjected.

"That's a direct quote." Julian looked apologetic. He thumbed toward Caleb. "The local police department has been asked to completely take over the investigation." He gave Madi a pointed look. "Which Caleb wasn't happy about, to say the least."

Madi's stomach twisted.

"We're going to be questioned again," she realized.

"Sadly, that was going to happen no matter what," her mom said. "This town is small enough that no one can be that easily dismissed." She grabbed Madi's hand and squeezed. "Even when they're innocent."

Madi knew that was true but that didn't stop that stomach twist from mixing in with a little dread. She might not have killed Loraine but she'd still been complicit in a lie to the department. Her brothers' department. If all of this blew back it wouldn't just hurt her and her child, it would hurt the rest of her family, too.

And Julian.

Even with the table between them Madi felt him against her skin. Felt his body heat enveloping hers, comforting and strong. Immovable. Was it what she wanted now or just a memory dredged up thanks to worry and pregnancy hormones?

Once upon a time, Julian Mercer had made her feel safe.

"What about Hidden Hills?" she asked. Jenna had taken over locking up, but Madi realized now with more than a dose of regret that she had lost sight of what would happen next with the inn. "What about the other guest, Ray? I completely spaced about him in all of the chaos."

"Desmond went to relieve Jenna this morning," her mother answered. "As for Ray, he's in a cabin at the retreat."

Under normal circumstances, Madi would have been riled up. After announcing her pregnancy to her mother, her concern that she was competing with her family had been pushed low on her priority list. Now Madi was just grateful. Hidden Hills *was* a crime scene after all.

"Good," Madi said. "Though I still want to head over there myself."

Caleb was shaking his head before he ended his call.

"You can't go snooping through it yet."

"I don't want to *snoop*," Madi countered. "All of my clothes and things are there!"

Caleb rolled his eyes and addressed their mother.

"Jazz just got out of a meeting with Declan and two detectives from the local PD. Like we thought, they want to conduct interviews all over again, plus add a few. Declan offered the conference room in the department for convenience's sake and they finally agreed. It probably would look better if we all headed there now. Show that we're not trying to avoid anything."

Madi's gut twisted. Her mother stood, Julian rising in sync. Madi had a little more trouble. Her baby belly was relatively small, yet she still wasn't graceful.

"Let me run and get some things from the house and I'll be ready," her mother said. Caleb started to dial another number.

"I need to touch base with Nina and Desmond."

Julian reached out and helped Madi stand. His hand was warm, strong. Distracting. She was grateful when he looked down at his phone and not into her eyes when she was standing tall again.

"I need to call Chance," he explained.

"Chance? Your friend from Alabama?"

He nodded. Then his voice was low.

"He's the only person who could prove I wasn't with you before the body was found."

Madi felt her eyes widen but he didn't give her more than that. Instead she was left next to the table as the three of them scattered. It made her feel even more helpless.

And that was when it hit her.

A detail she hadn't focused on fully yet.

Something that had fallen through the cracks as the shock had paved over everything.

The shotgun.

She hadn't heard the shot that ended Loraine's life.

Someone hadn't just killed the socialite; they'd done it somewhere other than Hidden Hills.

Why would someone go through the trouble of bringing her back?

And putting her in Madi's bed?

Madi rubbed her stomach, chewing on the thought. It was a sour taste.

"I think we need to go over a few more things before we head out," Julian said after a couple of minutes. He sidled up to her, close enough again that she was enveloped by his scent. "Especially if we're about to be put through the wringer."

"Agreed."

The main house's back door swung open. Madi's mother hurried over to them, brow creased.

"This is probably more madness," Madi muttered.

"Someone's driving up the road but I don't recognize the truck," her mother said without preamble. It was enough to pull Caleb off his call. They turned as the sound of crunching gravel preceded an old black two-door Ford. Madi didn't recognize the vehicle, either. It came to a stop on the side of the road between the houses.

The man, however, she did recognize.

Madi's triplet telepathy flared to life. Caleb gave her the briefest of glances before squaring his shoulders. Their mother lost any and all signs of a polite, hospitable woman. Madi felt ice in her veins.

"What's wrong?" Julian asked at her ear.

Madi didn't have time to hold up the walls around her that guarded her. Not when *he* was walking across the grass toward them, badge glaring at them from his belt.

"Remember last time you were here and I told you that everyone in the county likes at least one of us Nashes?" she said, voice low. "So much so it's like a running joke in town?"

"Yeah."

"You're looking at the one man who hates all of us."

"The feeling's mutual," Caleb threw in despite the distance between them. Their mother didn't deny either accusation.

Julian's jaw hardened.

"Why?" he asked.

Madi didn't take her eyes off the approaching man. She hadn't told Julian about her past—why she had the scar on her cheek—but now wasn't the time to be coy with the information. She had to bullet-point it for him. He needed to be on the same page when it came to the man.

"When my brothers and I were eight, a man abducted us from a park. We were held for three days in a cabin in the woods before we managed to escape. The guy who took and held us got away, never to be seen again. My dad had a theory that someone paid him to take us for whatever reason, but died before he could prove it." There was steel in her next words. "You're looking at the only suspect my dad ever had."

THE CHANGE IN all three Nashes was more than alarming. Madi's hurried explanation of why was enraging. Julian pictured the scar across her face and replayed the small limp that Desmond walked with. He'd never asked about either but now wondered if both were born from that trauma.

The man of the hour closed the distance between himself and their group.

The mood hadn't just gone cold, it had plummeted into arctic waters. Even the Nash matriarch was as stiff as a board.

"Good morning, Nash family," the man greeted. He smiled but it was as off as the surrounding mood. His eyes roamed to Julian. "And guest." He reached his hand out, bypassing Caleb and Dorothy until he got to Julian. "I don't think we've met. I'm Christian Miller. Lead detective from the Kilwin Police Department."

Julian shook. The man's grip was a little too tight.

"Julian Mercer. Nice to meet you."

Miller didn't seem to share the sentiment.

He stepped back to face them as a group.

Julian placed him in his upper fifties. He was bald on top but had a salt-and-pepper beard shaved close. It highlighted the frown that had deepened at the sight of them. He wasn't a big man, but there was a severity to him. He was also easy to read. He held no love for the people he was around and they held no love for him.

Not that Julian expected anything less after the bomb that Madi had just dropped. That was one more conversation he wanted to have with the woman with balled fists at his side.

"Well, I'm assuming the sheriff has already informed you about us handling the case," he started, voice gruff. "I just want to let y'all know there are no hard feelings. This investigation is going to be conducted in a professional manner. That's what Mrs. Wilson deserves and that's what she's going to get." His eyes wandered to Madi's. Julian had never seen her so rigid. It inspired an almost primal reaction within him.

He wanted to protect Madi. He wanted to protect all of the Nashes. Even if he didn't understand all the nuances to the situation, Julian knew beyond a shadow of a doubt that Christian Miller was a threat. And he had made a career out of assessing and dealing with those.

"So…" The detective's demeanor changed. He smirked and waved between them. "I know how tight this family can be so we're going to go ahead and have Madeline come with me. I think it's a damn shame how this case has already been handled. The department shouldn't have even responded. All it did was give you time to get your stories straight. Really a damn shame, if you ask me. It's just another example of how the Nashes always seem to get their way. That stops today."

"I'm not going anywhere with you."

Julian wouldn't have believed the words came from Madi had he not seen her speak them. Each held a knife's edge, sharp and biting.

The detective's demeanor changed yet again. This time there was no smirk.

"A woman was found in your bed, killed by your father's shotgun, which was found on your coffee table," he said. "A witness claimed to have heard you talking about wanting that same woman dead several times that day. The call that you claimed not to have made to the victim was found in your phone log. And let's not forget the glaring detail that everyone seems to have glazed over because you just happen to be pregnant—" His eyes narrowed to almost slits. A new wave of tension moved across the Nash matriarch and her children. Julian took one small step forward. "You have violence in you, Madeline. You may smile, you may say nice things, but at the end of the day I know you're more than capable of doing exactly what was done. And this time, this family is going to pay the consequences for their actions. Pregnant or not."

Caleb looked ready to lunge. So did Dorothy. Julian moved closer before either could.

"Watch out there, Detective," Julian ground out. "I think your bias is showing."

The man laughed, an embittered sound.

"If I were you, buddy, I'd cool my jets," he said. "You just so happened to be the perfect alibi for the Nash daughter, but I'd bet my badge that everything you've said so far has been a lie. You want to know what else I think? I think you didn't come to see her at all. You just happened to be in the right place at the wrong time." His voice dipped into a sharpness that rivaled Madi's. "That's when she convinced you to lie. That's when you broke the law. And that is what I intend to prove."

Caleb started to rally but Julian spoke over him.

"You're right. I didn't come to see Madi."

The innkeeper placed a hand over her pregnant stomach, eyes wide in confusion. Julian hoped what he said next wouldn't hurt their case more than it helped. Then again, whether or not they would admit it out loud, everyone in that yard was nearing the edge of a cliff. One that they could be pushed off at any second, whether it be by a murder with no leads, a rich and recently widowed husband on the warpath, or a lawman with a grudge. If they didn't start building a bridge soon, what hope did they have to get on the other side of it all?

Julian might have lied about the alibi but Madi was innocent. He was going to help her the best he could. So he aimed to control the one part of the investigation that he could at the moment.

If Detective Miller was accusing him of being a stranger, then Julian needed to correct him.

He looked the man right in the eye and spoke clearly.

"I came to see my daughter."

In front of God and everyone there, Julian placed his hand over Madi's. Both were resting against her stomach.

Against their daughter.

Chapter Six

Madi had to hand it to her family—their poker faces were fantastic.

No one, not even her triplet brothers, had known who the father of her unborn child was. She'd decided not to tell anyone after realizing she might not ever see Julian again. It had been the sore spot between her and her mother. Dorothy Nash was a fierce protector when it came to her children but she couldn't protect them without all of the details. Madi had taken a stand after another round of questioning from her mother and brothers. She would tell them who it was when the time was right.

Now? So close to a man she'd loathed for years and hurtling toward an investigation that made her look like a murderer? It certainly didn't feel like the right time.

Though it was effective.

Detective Miller hadn't been able to hide his surprise as well as her mother and Caleb had. His

smug and righteous attitude had zipped away, replaced by a critical look split among her, Julian
and the stomach they were both touching.

"You're the father," Detective Miller said.

Julian nodded.

"And I'd be happy to confirm that during my
interview." He dropped his hand from her stomach. Its heat went with it, leaving Madi in want.
His admission that he was the father had shifted
something inside her. Sure, she'd known—and for
much longer than him—yet now it felt different.
It made the guarded part of her heart feel even
more vulnerable than it had.

Julian motioned to the detective's truck. His
expression wasn't giving anything away.

"Which I think it would be more professional
to do at the department instead of out here in the
yard," he continued. "So why don't we all head
that way now? That SUV parked at the main
house is mine. You can follow us there if it'll make
you feel better, but unless you have something to
charge her with right now, I think it'll be better
for all of us if Madi rides with me."

Julian was absolutely thrumming with authority. One second he'd been the quiet yet hard-to-
miss man at her side. Now his words carried more
power than anything Detective Miller had said.
It had affected her mother and Caleb, too. The
first had loosened her shoulders; the latter had

unclenched his fists. With a few sentences Julian had managed to flip the tables.

Now it was Miller who was on unstable ground.

"Fine," he said, not at all sounding like it was fine. "I'll follow you but if you do anything, and I mean anything, that seems even remotely suspicious, I'll call the whole county on you. On all of you."

He didn't give them another word. Madi and her family didn't speak, either. No matter how badly she wanted to say a few words that might have made Grandma Nash roll over in her grave.

Caleb was the first to break their formation.

He turned to Madi. His eyes dropped to her stomach before going to Julian.

"Was that the truth?"

Madi nodded. There was no point in keeping the secret any longer.

Caleb seemed to assess Julian with new attention. What conclusion he came to, Madi couldn't tell.

"The longer we wait to go to the department, the more ammo we give Miller," he added. His face twisted in anger. "I get why the case was moved to another agency but giving it to him? That's on the far side of the professional spectrum. But don't worry. Declan and I will fix this."

Her mother still hadn't moved. Madi couldn't tell if she was angry at Miller's sudden reappearance or if there was something else moving beneath the surface.

"Mom?" she tried. "Do you want to ride with us?"

Dorothy Nash kept her expression unreadable.

"No, dear, but thank you. I think I'll take my own car."

Madi tried to smile, tried to give her something that would make everything better, but there wasn't much she could do. She felt no joy in the wake of one of the Nash family's ghosts of tragedies past.

Julian and Madi went straight to his SUV. Detective Miller lurked in his truck, waiting. Julian was a cool cucumber. Only belatedly did Madi wonder if that was because of his military experience.

"I bet you're sorry you came to visit me this time, huh?" Madi asked after they were moving down the ranch's main road.

Julian shrugged, eyes ahead.

"Sometimes things happen," he said. "You can either hang on for the ride or jump off before it gets anywhere good. You just have to adapt."

"Adapt," Madi repeated. "That's a word I used to hear a lot." Absently she brushed her fingers across the scar on her cheek. Most days she forgot it was there; others it was impossible to pretend it wasn't. "Adapting or not, Miller isn't going to back down," she added on. "There's too much bad blood there."

"And he's not making it a secret that he holds some serious anger for your family. I can't imagine it's ethical for him to be the lead investigator."

Madi sighed. Her ankles were starting to swell. The heat never helped.

"I need to go to Hidden Hills after the interviews. If I'm not charged with anything, that is. Everything I own is in that house."

Julian nodded to the road.

"We'll get you there."

Madi didn't like that his words made her feel better, but there was no denying that they did. She let out another long, deep breath and rubbed a hand over her stomach. There was so much they could talk about that it muted them. Silence filled the vehicle.

Which topic would they even focus on?

The murder? The lying? Their reunion? Their daughter?

The weather?

"Madi?"

They were moving down the county road toward town. The sun was shining. Madi longed for a normal summer day. Swimsuits, sun and carefree fun. No mystery. No Miller. No death. "Madi," he repeated again. "Something's happening."

His eyes were on the rearview mirror. Madi

turned, worry flooding her system. Caleb had broken their caravan. He sped around them, flashers on. Detective Miller had his on, too, but was motioning through his window for them to pull over. When they were on the shoulder, Miller stopped on the road next to them.

He didn't get out.

"You go straight to the department right now or so help me God I'll send a manhunt after you two," he yelled. "Got it?"

"Got it."

Julian didn't get a chance to ask what was wrong. The detective floored it after Caleb. Madi's mother pulled up behind them, brow knit. She threw up her hand in confusion. Madi shrugged.

"Something happened," Julian said. He steered them back onto the road and turned on the radio. "I don't like this."

"It seems to be a theme lately."

Madi turned on the radio and searched until she was on the local station. The hair started to stand up on the back of her neck.

The Morning Rundown radio show with hosts Micah and Calhoun should have been rolling through the usual spiel with prank calls, talk of viral videos, relationship blunders and fart jokes. Instead, Micah's high-pitched, nasal voice was strained.

"…avoid County Road 11. Take Jackson Road

to the highway to get to Kilwin or reroute through Rockport Landing. Again, if you plan on using County Road 11, detour instead. The road has been shut down due to what appears to be a large motor vehicle fire. Authorities are currently blocking the road and trying to get a handle on the situation. Do not take County Road 11."

Calhoun, his cohost, spoke in a more reserved fashion than her normal radio persona. A car fire didn't seem to warrant the change.

"For those of you who have called in about it, thank you. We'll be back after this commercial break."

Madi tilted her head to the side a fraction, confused.

"Surely that's not where Caleb and Miller are going," she said. "County Road 11 is on the opposite side of town from us. The department is closer than we are. Plus, Kilwin's volunteer fire station would be, too."

"Maybe they went out on another call," Julian pointed out. "Or maybe the deputies at the fire needed more help?"

Madi didn't hear any conviction in his voice.

"Maybe." She didn't hear any conviction in hers, either.

When they got to the sheriff's department, that niggling feeling of dread was confirmed. It was not as simple as not enough hands on deck or another call that needed their response.

Desmond met them at the front stairs. He was in one of his best suits, his black Stetson on and his cell phone in his hand. He was also rattled. It was a look that set Madi's already-fraying nerves to ribbons. When he set eyes on Madi, the concern was palpable.

"Where were you just now?" he asked without segue.

Madi was taken aback by his demanding tone.

"I—I was at the ranch. Talking to Christian Miller. Why?"

Des sagged in relief. Which was telling in itself. He disliked Miller just as she did. The detective's reappearance in their lives should have had more of an impact.

"Thank goodness," he said. "I didn't think you did it but was afraid you wouldn't have an alibi this time."

"Come again?" she asked just as Julian repeated, "This time?"

Des motioned them to follow him.

"I want to make sure as many people see you as possible, just in case. Declan said for us to meet in the conference room for the interviews but let's go ahead and get in there now. Then I'll explain."

Their mother pulled up and with her they followed him inside the faded and chipped brick building with a collective and mounting worry. Declan was the sheriff; Caleb was a long-standing detective. Desmond might not have been law enforcement but his work and charm had made connections with almost everyone in town. Madi knew the faces that turned toward them as they passed. She'd been to their weddings, given their kids birthday presents, talked to them in the aisles at the grocery store, knew their embarrassing stories from adolescence and could give at least one fun fact about each. She knew the department and the people who worked inside its walls.

Yet as several pairs of eyes set on her, Madi had no idea what her friends were thinking.

What had happened?

The conference room was right off the bull pen, visible through the glass windows that lined the shared wall. Des didn't close the blinds over them but he did turn his face away.

"What's going on, Des?" their mother asked, hands wrapped around her cell phone like it was a lifeline. Madi fought the urge to wrap her own hand around Julian's.

"Does it have to do with the car fire out on County Road 11?" Madi followed up.

Des nodded.

"Yes and no. It wasn't just a car fire." He placed his hat on the table in the center of the room. Madi sank into one of the chairs. Everyone else remained standing. "Carl Smith, the county coroner, was transporting Loraine's body to Kilwin this morning. Lee Holloway, the junior detective working at the police department, was accompanying him. He made a distress call yelling that someone was trying to run them off the road." Des paused and looked back at Madi. "He said it was a blonde woman."

Madi felt her eyes widen.

"But there are more blonde women in this world than Madi," Julian said. "They can't think it was her anyway. I'm assuming this all happened while Detective Miller had an eye on us."

"Which is the only good news about this whole situation," Des continued. "Miller may hate us, but that hate can't put Madi in two places at once."

"What happened to Carl and the detective?" their mother asked. "Are they okay?"

Des's face became even more grim.

"The van was engulfed last I heard...and there was a body inside. Not just Loraine's. That's all I overheard in here before someone said you all had pulled up."

Madi shook her head.

"I don't understand what's going on. We went from normal to crazy in less than a day!"

Julian agreed with the sentiment.

"Whatever is happening, it's nothing good."

"OH GOD, I can't believe you shot me!"

The man wrapped the strip of his shirt he'd torn off around the bullet hole in his hand. He'd already gotten sick just looking at it, never mind the pain. The man who had taken the shot was glaring at him above his duct tape gag. His look promised more than pain if he ever got loose from the cuffs around his wrists. Or the binding around him.

He wouldn't.

And if he did? Well, where would he go?

"Make sure you wrap it up tight."

The sweet voice often caught him off guard. It preceded a woman he believed was made from fire and steel. Looks were definitely deceiving with her.

But again, that was the point.

"Do you think they bought it?" he asked, trying to knot the cloth tighter.

The woman laughed. It was dark and calculated. How he loved the sound.

"They better have. I don't want to stick my neck out anymore. This was the last big splash." The smile crept across her lips, resembling a lioness preparing to go on a hunt. Despite the pain he was in, it rallied him. "But if they still don't think Little Miss Perfect is capable of such horrors, then we'll just have to convince them. Until then—"

She picked the gun up and walked over to their

captive. He lashed against the ropes around him. There wasn't anything he could really do beyond that.

"Have you heard the phrase 'an eye for an eye'?" she asked. She walked her index and middle fingers down his chest. The duct tape muffled his anger. "It's a really big thing for me, an eye for an eye. It's a principle I learned at an early age. One I truly believe in. One that applies to everyone." She stood back to full height, moved around his back and pressed the gun against the palm of his hand. He thrashed around again. It did nothing but make her smile grow. "No matter if they're a young man wearing a badge or a pregnant innkeeper."

She pulled the trigger.

Not even the duct tape could muffle the man's scream.

Chapter Seven

Julian hung by the conference room door. His legs were stiff from standing in one spot but he wasn't going to sit. The closest available chairs were in the lobby. That was too far away.

He wasn't going to leave Madi. Even now with the door shut between them, Julian couldn't help but feel uneasy. He wasn't going to lengthen that distance.

"She's a tough one, you know." Dorothy Nash walked up with a small smile. She motioned to the door. "Madeline may look fragile on occasion but I tell you what, sometimes she gives all of my boys a run for their money."

Julian hadn't had time for a one on one with any of the Nashes, Madi included, since they'd made their way into the department. He knew it was only a matter of time before the pregnancy was brought up. Along with why he hadn't been around through it. Still, he wasn't going to be the one who dived into that topic first. Not with everything going on.

"That I don't doubt," he said.

Dorothy took the spot next to him, lining up her shoes inside the large square tile. After her statement and interview with another Kilwin PD detective named Devereux, she had moved to the sheriff's personal office for privacy. Declan was at the scene with most of the department, but those left behind hadn't made one peep of protest as she'd gone in and shut the door behind her. It was clear that, despite everything that had happened in the last twenty-four hours, it took more to lessen the respect for the Nash matriarch.

She crossed her arms over her chest and let out a long breath. They had been at the Wildman County Sheriff's Department for several hours. Two of those had been spent waiting, wondering what was going on. Then Detective Devereux had shown up. Julian had read the tension in the man well before he spoke. Worry had folded a line into his forehead; his eyes had jumped around as he took them all in, unable to settle.

"Detective Holloway appears to have been taken by force by whoever attacked the coroner's van," he had said, barely able to hide the anger and concern there. "Our only suspect is a blonde woman." He had focused on Madi, and Julian felt relief when there didn't seem to be any malice toward her. "Detective Miller puts all of you within eyesight before and during the incident."

He'd pulled out a small spiral notebook. "Does anyone have any information they'd like to share before individual interviews?"

The room had quieted as Julian, Madi, Dorothy and Desmond had shaken their heads. No one knew what was going on, local or not.

Past that, their interviews had started with Dorothy before ending with Madi, who was still inside now. Julian was glad Detective Miller wasn't around. His questions might have delved further into their lie. As far as Julian could read through Detective Devereux's body language, the investigator believed what he had to say.

Julian hoped the same went for Madi.

"Madi said you were here before?" Dorothy's words were low but pointed. "I mean here in Overlook?"

"Yes ma'am, but then I had to leave." His answer was curt, but he didn't know the extent of what Dorothy was privy to when it came to Madi and the pregnancy. A thought that made his skin crawl. Everyone here had known about her pregnancy while he had been clueless. What if he had decided to keep driving instead of taking his detour?

Would Madi have been sent to prison?

Would he have ever had a chance to meet his daughter?

These questions had been springing up too often in the last few hours. He was going to talk to

Madi at length about everything when things died down. That was for sure. Until then he wanted to keep all of his cards close to his chest.

"You had to go back home?"

Julian shook his head. So Dorothy didn't know about him being in the military. Which meant Madi hadn't told her mother about him.

Or the fact that she'd been the one to end things between them. No matter how short their time together had been.

"I had to get things squared away for a job after my next deployment ended, which it just did."

Dorothy's eyes widened in surprise at the information. She didn't voice it. Instead she let out another sigh.

"Well, I suppose we're all lucky for your sense of timing," she said. "Madi and the baby don't need this stress. No one does."

Her expression darkened and the conversation stalled out. Julian was good at silences, so he lounged in theirs until, finally, the door behind them opened. Detective Devereux with his flame-red hair came into view, looking more world-weary than he had when he'd first walked into the department.

He wasn't a local in Overlook but he knew to address Dorothy with respect. Another deviation from what might have been had Miller grilling them.

"For now you all are free to go, but I'd appreciate it if no one left town and you all kept your phones on you just in case we need to get ahold of you." He moved out of the doorway so Madi could make her way out, too. She smiled but it was tight—channeling her customer service skills, Julian had no doubt. Devereux didn't care one way or the other. His gaze swept the room behind them. He found no relief in what he saw. "You can return back to your home," he said to Madi. "We have everything we needed from the crime scene." Then he was charging across the room, phone up to his ear.

Julian felt for the man. He was worried about the missing detective—his colleague, most likely his friend. He also knew the overwhelming worry of leaving a man behind. How it could drive someone to great lengths to get him back.

Which was why Julian directed Madi and her mother out of the department and to their vehicles as fast as he could. It was easy to see the department and Kilwin PD were looking for someone to blame. He didn't want that urgency to make them point fingers at someone they shouldn't.

Still, both women hesitated in the parking lot. Madi cut her glance between Julian and her mother.

"How you doing, Ma?"

Dorothy surprised him by cracking a smile.

"Oh, you know me. Focusing on one thing I can do and not all the things I can't."

Madi rubbed her hand across the older woman's back. Julian had noticed the tension between them earlier and hadn't been surprised it was there. Dorothy had been a sore topic when he was at Hidden Hills all those months ago. Yet for that one moment, he saw nothing but love between the two.

"Dad might have talked a lot, but that was my favorite piece of advice." She turned her smile to Julian. "There's never enough time to do everything, so focus on the one thing you can."

He nodded. "Definitely good advice."

Madi dropped her hand, along with her smile. She glanced at the department behind them.

"I need to go back to the inn and see how everything looks," she said, voice hard. Resolute. "If it's all good then I'll call Ray and, if he's willing, tell him to come back to his cabin."

A look Julian couldn't place flashed across Dorothy's face but she nodded.

"Let me know what he says. I can help."

They hugged and Dorothy said goodbye. She hung back where only Julian could hear her. Her words held more of a wallop than he cared to admit.

"You make sure nothing happens to my baby, Mr. Mercer. Yours, too."

MADI FELT DISMAL. Take away the stress and confusion of what had happened to Loraine and the missing detective, and take away the mountain of handsome that was the man driving her home, and there was still a fact that blared like an unending alarm. She was almost seven months pregnant.

Her ankles were swollen. She was hot and hungry. Halfway through the questioning she'd caught a whiff of Julian's cologne and spent the next half hour trying to not be as turned on as she was. But, as she'd been learning the last few months, being pregnant was a wild, unpredictable ride. It was marked with things such as hormones running rampant, love that knew no bounds and stretch marks. My goodness, the stretch marks.

Now as they stood in the doorway of her bedroom at Hidden Hills, Madi waited for her hormones to knock her down. To pull out tears that would rival the creek flowing through her property. Yet nothing came.

"She was in your bedroom?" Julian asked, moving past her to the coffee table in the living space. It was cleaned off.

"Yeah, on the bed."

Madi cringed as the image of the body thrown across the foot of the bed flashed through her mind. She moved back to the hallway like she could escape it and what had happened. Julian went in the opposite direction. He stepped into the bedroom and cracked the door behind him. Madi didn't try to see around it.

After a minute or two he came out, done with his inspection.

"Uh, how attached are you to your mattress?" Madi cringed.

"I didn't even think about it with everything going on. Is it that bad?"

"Let's just say that I'd feel more comfortable getting that thing out of there while you're somewhere else." He shook his head. "It's not pretty."

Madi sighed.

"I don't think I could sleep on it again, anyways." Anger surged from the tips of her toes out to the roots of her hair. It was so sudden and violent that she took a step farther back into the hallway, as if her body were trying to keep Julian from seeing that side of her before her brain had the chance to stop the words that poured from her mouth. "Whoever killed Loraine did it somewhere else and then brought her here! To my home, into *my bed*, and for what? To make it look like I killed her? Why? Why do this?" That anger burned holes in her calm. Tears leaked through. She balled her hands. "I didn't like Loraine but I didn't want *that*. Why would someone do this?"

Julian walked over to her slowly. Each step was calculated. Every movement controlled. It only made Madi feel even worse. She was the one who needed to get back some control.

"We'll figure this out," he said. "But first, let's tackle what we can." He tried on a grin. It was weirdly reassuring. "I'm sure I'm not the only one who needs to eat something. Come with me to the kitchen?"

Julian held out his elbow. Madi wiped at her tears, then took it. His skin was warm against hers. A Band-Aid to hold closed the wound. His presence was something Madi had longed for ever since he left. Even before she'd found out she was pregnant.

There was something about the man that calmed her. Yet at the same time, excited her beyond reason.

Why had she turned him away?

Madi felt the heat of shame slither up her neck. She knew why.

It was the same reason she'd never had a long-term relationship in her thirty years of life. The same reason her friendships were limited to Jenna and few others. The same reason she wanted to deal in a profession that brought in strangers who *left* as strangers.

The same reason she was terrified of being a mother.

Madi hadn't just been hurt as a child, she'd been broken. Some of those pieces that had been shattered would never be put back together again. She didn't want them to be.

You can't do everything, so just focus on the one thing you can.

Michael Nash had said that countless times but it was only now, walking arm in arm with the father of her child, through the inn that was her home, that Madi finally realized she'd taken the advice further than she'd realized.

Instead of moving on from her fear, she'd just removed herself from the world as best she could.

Yet somehow, fear had found her again.

This time, it brought death, too.

Chapter Eight

Nathan Wilson was staying in a hotel in Kilwin. Ray had opted to stay at the Wild Iris Retreat on the ranch until the next day. Jenna had also had a long night before and would wait until further notice to come in. As for the Nash brothers? Julian didn't know yet.

Which left him sitting across from Madi, eating peanut butter and jelly sandwiches in silence.

She had her feet up on a chair in the eat-in part of the kitchen, gaze firmly out the window. It looked into the backyard, but in the waning light after dusk, the view was slowly being snuffed out. The change sent shadows that dulled the strands of gold splayed out across her back. For once they weren't braided. Another change in a long list of differences between this visit and his last.

Julian prided himself on noticing details. The little things. The small movements. The subtle shifts. It had been his bread and butter in his military career, helping him better the world by understanding it just a bit more than most.

Right now that skill was telling him three things, just as it had the first time he'd seen Madi months ago.

One, Madi was uncomfortable and not just in the emotional sense. Every few minutes she would readjust. The briefest flash of annoyance would move across her expression. She'd stroke her stomach and then settle again. Only to do it all over again. Julian couldn't deny every time it happened his concern went from normal to all-out alert. He came from a small family. Loving parents and a sister, Bethany, only one year younger than him. He'd never had the chance to be around someone pregnant before. Certainly not six months along and wrapped up in a murder investigation. He didn't know what was normal in either situation, never mind combined.

Two, something had changed between their walk from Madi's room to the kitchen. Julian had felt it through their touch and then seen it in her face. Or, really, hadn't seen it. Madi had gone from a rush of emotions to closed off. First she'd been angry at the senseless act of violence, then she had cried. Even now Julian could feel the need to comfort her pulsing through him. The tears that had traveled down her beautiful tanned skin had only reminded him that as much as he wanted to, he couldn't protect her from everything. That included whatever had prompted her to surround herself with the invisible walls that were keeping him out. Julian couldn't blame her for her caution, but that didn't mean he had to like the idea that she had retreated away from him. Again.

And the third thing he knew without a doubt was that, despite the time that had passed since they'd seen each other, he still found her impossibly beautiful. Exhaustion? Stress? Worry? They might have changed the way she was holding herself but they hadn't changed the way Julian marveled at her. There was an effortless way about her beauty. It drew him in months ago, just as it beckoned to him now. Julian wanted to reach across the small table and tuck a strand of her hair behind her ear. To look into those sky blue eyes before pressing his lips to hers. Before he could police those thoughts, parts of him started to wake up in excitement. Memories of doing that, and more, started to flood back in.

It wasn't like the first day he'd met her all over again, wondering what she felt like. Tasted like.

Those were questions that had turned into memories and he'd be lying if he said he didn't want to revisit those moments.

Even after the fact that she had kept something from him. Rather, someone. A daughter.

Which would make him a father.

Julian prided himself on understanding and recognizing the small things in life. The details that made up every day. Yet, when he thought about his future before he'd met Madi? Before he'd found out he was going to be a father?

Well, he'd imagined thousands of little details that his future might be made up of and having a daughter hadn't been one of those details. At least, not like this.

He wanted the job with Chance to be the start of growing roots, of staying still. Eventually he knew that would turn into his own family. A wife. Children.

But now the details he'd imagined of his future were different. Not only had he found Madi after months of being apart, he'd found more questions than answers surrounding her.

Did she expect him to leave again?

Did she want him to?

Did she regret that he was the father?

Sitting across from the golden-haired innkeeper as she stroked her pregnant stomach, Julian found that despite the questions he had there was one answer that was clear.

He would love and protect his daughter for the rest of his life.

No matter what.

The realization rocked through him in such a profound way he nearly said it out loud.

Madi, unaware of his influx of paternal love, shifted in her chair again. She winced, took the last bite of her sandwich, and then stroked her stomach again. This time she kept her hand resting there.

Julian also realized he wasn't the only one trying to protect someone.

He opened his mouth to speak, but Madi beat him to it.

"I don't share this story a lot, or really at all, but everyone in town knows it." Her gaze swung to his. "It's only fair I catch you up."

Madi let out an unmistakably defeated breath.

"Okay," he said. "I'm listening."

For a moment Julian didn't think she'd continue, but then she looked out of the window again and did just that.

"When Desmond, Caleb and I were eight we sneaked out to a local park. We were bored and you know how mob mentality works? Well, that was us when we were together. Triplet terrors." She smiled. It was brief. "The park was really just trails in the woods with a picnic area thrown in the middle. Nothing too fancy but, for us, it was a fun place to play. That day, we decided to play hide-and-seek. Des and I went to go hide while Caleb counted… For the life of me, to this day, I can't remember what I first thought when I saw the man. I just remember screaming."

Julian's hands fisted beneath the table. It was hard to hold his anger in. It wouldn't help eight-year-old Madi or her siblings now.

"He grabbed me before I could run. When Des and Caleb showed up he had a gun on me and told us that we were coming with him. All three of us." She shook her head. "My dad was a detective at the sheriff's department, before that a deputy for years, just like his dad. He'd made sure that all of us knew that there were bad people in the world and if those bad people ever tried to take any of us anywhere to fight like hell."

"Chances of survival go down tremendously once a person gets into a car while being kidnapped," he stated, already knowing the statistic. Madi nodded.

"As soon as he said the words, that was all I could hear," she continued. "Dad just telling us over and over again to fight. To escape. To not be taken even if there was a risk we'd get hurt. So I did what I could." She fisted her hand but didn't mimic any movement. "Caleb called it a throat punch but I just hit the first thing I could with how he held me. I didn't even realize it was his throat until he let me go. But it wasn't enough." Madi turned her head. She ran a finger across the scar on her cheekbone. "He pistol-whipped me. And that's all she wrote on my end. It knocked me out cold and left a constant reminder."

Julian swore. There was no way he could hide his disgust for a man who would hit a child. Madi waited until he was done to continue. She didn't turn toward the window again but her eyes were averted. Julian recognized the past glazing over them as she replayed what had happened for him.

"Apparently this incensed the boys. The man shot at them to keep them away as he tried to get his bearings back. A bullet grazed Caleb's arm pretty deep, blood went everywhere, or so I'm told. That only revved Desmond up even more. He managed to jump on the man. That didn't work out, either. He was thrown to the ground, where the man then stomped on Des's leg and broke it. And just like that, he was three for three. He took me to the car and the boys followed, Caleb dragging Des along, both bloody and broken. They didn't want to leave me." Madi paused, collecting herself. Julian realized his adrenaline was surging, building along with his rage at their attacker. She cleared her throat after a moment and finished the story. "He used the threat of hurting me to get the boys to comply with being blindfolded and to behave as he took us to a cabin out in the woods near the town limits. He locked us in the basement apartment. Three beds, a bathroom and no earthly idea as to the why of it all. He held us for three days."

Julian shook his head.

"Who the hell would do that?" He seethed. "You were children."

Madi let out a long breath.

"The man only ever spoke to us to threaten us to behave. He'd bring us food, tell us he'd hurt Desmond even more if we tried to escape, and then would leave. So we listened... Until we didn't."

Julian had thought the end of the story was nearing before but now he could read the ramp up to the climax in Madi's expression. Memories bled through people's guarded walls sometimes, even if they didn't want them to. Madi couldn't hide the anger, anguish and defiance that flashed across her face in quick succession as she spoke again.

"Des was in so much pain, even before we got into that basement. The man knew it and so we used that against him. Caleb and I yelled that Des had stopped breathing while Des tried his best to pretend. I can still remember how hard I cried, yelling out for him. Caleb at my side doing the same. One minute we were trying to fool the man, in the next I believed our lie. It helped us sell it. The second the man bent over Des to check on him, Caleb and I attacked. Then Des joined in. We worked like a unit, one mind between three little bodies, but it worked." She let out another, smaller breath. Relief, even though it was an old one, flitted over her causing some of the tension she'd been holding in her body to visibly lessen. In turn Julian felt himself calm down a little.

"We managed to lock him in the same place he'd locked us up before escaping into the woods," she continued. "A Good Samaritan found us and took us to the department."

"And the man?"

"Gone by the time Caleb led them back to the cabin. No clues. No leads to follow. My father tried his hardest to find him, even sacrificing his health through the years to do so. He passed away without uncovering anything."

"But he thought Detective Miller was involved?"

Julian had already disliked the man. That had only intensified hundredfold. Madi nodded.

"I never knew all the details," she said with regret. "Dad tried his hardest to keep us out of it, but whatever he found made him look at Miller. Eventually he stopped the accusations but you could tell he was still bothered by it." She took another deep breath. Her baby blues met his stare. "Which is the point of this story. The Nash triplet abduction is one of the most famous cases in Overlook history. The story of what happened has changed hands so many times that I've even been told about it with a few details completely wrong. It's like an urban legend here now...but before it evolved, it was a real, living and breathing mystery that ate at the town. When my dad started investigating Miller, it didn't matter that Dad didn't have evidence—it ate Miller up, too. His marriage ended, he left the department, left town and was only hired at the Kilwin Police Department after Dad passed. Whether or not he had anything to do with what happened—it didn't matter. The damage was more than done."

Her expression softened.

"Which is why I have to warn you about being with me. Being around me," she amended. "Our last name carries a lot of weight in this town, most of it good, but when it comes to Christian Miller? I'm sure he already has a cell with my name on it that he'll do anything to fill. I don't want you to get caught in his cross fire."

Relief, more powerful this time, seemed to deflate her rigidness. That was it. That was the end of her speech. There was still tension there but Madi appeared to have said her piece.

Julian understood why the woman had walls now...and she was giving him an out while she stayed behind them. Pain, trauma. They changed everything. A stone in the water with ripples moving out and touching every part of your life, even those around you.

Julian had seen pain. He understood trauma. He could empathize with how both affected a person and why Madi might need those invisible walls more than he needed to knock them down.

What he didn't understand was why Madi hadn't discussed her swollen belly or his daughter now or at any time in the last several months. A child was a game changer. One that didn't just affect Madi.

A daughter. His daughter.

With a start, sitting there in the kitchen, darkness creeping through the windows splaying shadows across the face of a beautiful woman, Julian realized he felt those words again. The meaning.

Pure, unyielding love slammed into Julian's chest like a Mack truck. No matter what happened between him and Madi, he knew, without a doubt, that he would be there for his child.

Sitting to his full height, he made sure to keep Madi's eye as he asked the question he'd been waiting to ask.

"Were you ever going to tell me about our daughter?"

To her credit, Madi didn't skip a beat. Her jaw hardened.

"I tried," she said, words clipped.

They also hit hard.

"You tried? How—" Julian cut himself off by swearing. One moment he was feeling a love unlike any he'd ever felt before, the next it was loathing. "I had to get a new number when I switched phones right before deployment. Which means the number I gave you was useless," She nodded. It was also a clipped movement. "And I didn't give you the new number," he finished.

She nodded again.

He felt like an idiot.

"It was hectic right before I left," he continued, knowing it was a lame excuse. He reached out for her hand just as she backed her chair up and stood. Still he finished the thought. "I should have called. I'm sorry."

Madi shook her head. Her expression had gone impassive again. The walls were up and reinforced.

"Why would you call me with a new number?" she asked, though it was rhetorical. "I'm the one who said we should go our separate ways. It's fine, really. I'm fine. This—" she motioned to her stomach "—was a surprise. One we're going to have to talk about at length, but…well…can that talk be tomorrow?" She smiled. It didn't reach her eyes. "If we don't get this inn under control, how am I supposed to get anything else under control?"

Before Julian could respond, her demeanor shifted.

"I mean, unless you want out of all of this? I know it's a lot of madness."

It was Julian's turn to stand. He made sure to keep eye contact this time, too.

"We can talk tomorrow," he said. "I'm not going anywhere."

Chapter Nine

The air had been cleared between Madi and Julian, at least somewhat. They were going to talk about the future in the future, and until then he was staying. Madi tried to keep the flutter of excitement in her stomach under control but the feeling lasted right up to Loraine and Nathan's room.

Julian whistled.

"It looks like a tornado tore through here."

Madi had to agree.

The guest suite was smaller than her personal one and, as a result, had only the necessary pieces of furniture. Those very same pieces had been either moved, flipped or otherwise disrupted. The desk chair was on its side, the dresser had a few of its drawers on the ground, the mattress had been mostly pulled off the bed and several towels had been thrown around the room.

"Looks like Nathan took some of his anger out in here," Julian said, not moving from the doorway.

Madi sighed.

"In his defense, he thinks I killed his wife." She went to the closest towel and tried to pick it up. It was like navigating around a yoga ball. A warm hand went to the small of her back right before Julian bent down and grabbed it instead. The contact was surprising. It made quelling the flutter in her chest even harder.

"I feel for him, I really do, but I'm glad he's staying somewhere else tonight." He went to the next towel and picked it up. "I don't want his misplaced aggression falling on you or this place. He needs to focus on figuring out who really killed her and why."

Madi's heart ached for the man. Loraine might have been a pill but Nathan had been nothing but kind and respectful to her. If not always on a business call.

"What I don't get is why she was killed in the first place," she said. "Here, I mean. It couldn't have been random. Someone brought her into the inn and into my room. Why? Was it a crime of opportunity and they brought her here because they panicked? Or did they follow her to Overlook and then do it when the time presented itself?" Madi felt like her head was going to explode with questions. "And what about the blonde woman who attacked the coroner's van? I'm not a detective but that's oddly coincidental since it had Loraine's body in it."

Julian moved around the room, picking up the rest of the towels. His lips were downturned in thought.

"And don't forget the cell phone bit."

"The cell phone bit?" she repeated.

"Your phone had a call to Loraine's phone logged in it. Plus Loraine's phone was placed on your table. And so was your father's shotgun, the supposed murder weapon."

Madi groaned. She pulled a section of her hair over her shoulder. Her fingers nimbly began to braid.

"Do you know how hard it is to keep all of this straight? Especially while you're nearing your third trimester?" she asked, voice raising. "One second everything is fine and the next I need a flowchart just to keep my sanity! Do you know the other day I had to make myself three cups of tea? Three! I kept forgetting where I put them or that I already had one cup in the other room. Finally I just gave up on trying to drink a whole one." She finished the braid and threw her hands wide. "Now I feel like I've been dropped into a really awful *Twilight Zone* episode where we find out at the very end that I did do it somehow!"

Julian closed the space between them, towels in his arms.

"I'm not almost seven months pregnant and I wouldn't mind a whiteboard to track all of this," he stated matter-of-factly. "This is a bizarre situation but one that, I'm sure, will make sense soon. Until then we can check off one fact we do know."

"What? That even though I just peed, I have to go again because this kid thinks my bladder is a trampoline?"

Julian snorted, then he was smirking.

"I was going to say that you didn't kill Loraine Wilson. But if it makes you feel better we can add 'baby uses bladder as a trampoline' to the list."

It shouldn't have helped her feel better but Madi couldn't deny that his words did the trick. If only enough to focus on the task at hand. Wordlessly the two moved around the room, straightening up. Julian took on the big-ticket items while Madi tackled the easier pieces. She'd already had a long talk with Desmond and the lawyer he hired about Hidden Hills. To play it safe she'd had to agree to shut the place down until the investigation was over. Not that she'd been thrown by that exactly, but it still had stung.

Hidden Hills wasn't just how she paid the bills, it was a purpose that focused her. That distracted her from the fears of being a mother and the loneliness that sometimes rocked through her.

Shutting down the inn, even temporarily, hurt. Plain and simple.

A heavy knock sounded on the front door as they finished up in the guest suite. The dull sound traveled up the stairs and right along Madi's spine. She shared a glance with Julian. He'd gone tense.

"Were you expecting anyone?"

"No, but I wouldn't be surprised if it were Miller. He didn't get a chance to grill us earlier."

Julian led the way down, careful to stay in front of her. That didn't change when he got to the door. Luckily, the face they saw on the other side was familiar.

"It's Des."

Julian opened the door and was met with a hardy handshake. Then Des was hugging her. It surprised Madi. While he could be an affectionate person, it was on occasion and usually not in front of strangers. Something must have happened. Her concern must have shown. When he pulled away, he sighed.

"Don't look at me like that. It's just been a long damn day."

Madi cut him some slack. She didn't push.

They went back into the kitchen while she made Des a sandwich. Or started to. There was no way to hide how tired she was and no way to avoid the obvious—she needed to rest. So when Julian took over the food preparations she caved.

"I'm going to go shower in the empty guest suite and, to be honest, probably lie down and watch some TV. My feet are killing me, my ankles are killing me and I'd really like to forget everything awful that has happened if only for a little while." She turned to Julian. "You have full rein of the inn." Then to Des, she added, "Let me know if anything happens, okay?"

They both nodded and went back to their conversation. They had switched to Julian's military experience. It was a subject she'd like to learn more about but just didn't have the stamina for currently. She wobbled out of the kitchen. Because that was how tired she was. Usually she could walk like a normal human being. Right now?

Penguin.

Through and through.

Just as she imagined herself waddling across the North Pole, Madi wondered how Julian saw her. And not just physically.

That flutter that had finally landed earlier took flight again.

A normal woman would have her mind on more pressing issues and yet...

Julian was there.

In her thoughts, swooping in without any rhyme or reason.

She might not be a normal woman, but it certainly didn't help that Julian wasn't your average man.

BLOOD SWIRLED AROUND the drain. It was an unsettling contrast against the clean white tile of the shower. Julian watched it for a while. The cut along his thigh looked back at him, angry. The edge of Madi's bed had been even angrier.

Julian was used to physical exertion but he'd never encountered such an infuriating bed in his life. He and Des had hit their legs against the frame several times before they'd even managed to wrestle the mattress off. Julian had seen Madi's legs before. They weren't covered in bruises and cuts, which only meant the innkeeper had some kind of secret for navigating the awkward piece of devil furniture.

But before he could complain too much about it, the dark stain had reminded him that there were much worse fates. They were quiet as they hauled the mattress out of the room and to the garage.

"I'd say we take it to the dump but it's pretty clear Detective Miller has an ax to grind," Julian had said after they pushed it up against one of the walls. "I don't want to give him any more ammo."

Des had nodded. Julian could see the same anger in his eyes that had been in Madi's.

"You're right about that," he had said, curt. Julian was about to get back to clearing out Madi's room but Des had more to say. Like his sister, Des's expression had become impassive, guarded. "I don't think Madi understands how…bad this situation is. I don't blame her for that. I know she's trying to keep it all together, trying to keep her stress levels down for the baby, but I don't think she's really thought about how it all looks."

"She didn't do it," Julian had to reiterate.

"But someone sure went through the trouble to make it look like she did, didn't they?" It had been a constant thought in the back of Julian's head. He nodded. "If you hadn't provided an alibi, things would have been astronomically worse. And if Miller hadn't been around when the unknown blonde woman was attacking the coroner's van?" Des had lowered his voice. "A murderer is out there and somehow they're involving Madi in their sick games. We have to keep her safe, Julian."

Julian hadn't even hesitated.

"We will."

It wasn't until just after nine that Des agreed to go home. Julian had gotten a little sleep that morning but he was pretty sure Des hadn't had a wink since Loraine had been found. He'd given Julian his number, told him to protect his sister again and driven off, leaving Julian to lock up. He had gone over every inch of the house—every door, every window—before finally going to the guest suite Madi was using.

There he'd found her, curled up on her side on the bed and fast asleep. Julian almost hated to turn the shower on in the next room. Then again, he was drenched in sweat and a bit of blood. Neither of which he thought she would appreciate. He was determined not to leave her side until the real killer was caught. He'd even left the door open to the bathroom, just enough to see Madi's sleeping face. It was comforting. More than it should have been.

He had realized that *complicated* didn't begin to explain his feelings for the woman. She had ended things before they had ever gotten started. She hadn't wanted to continue to see him. And now that she was pregnant with his child? From the vibes he was getting, that hadn't changed her mind.

So what would they be?

Ex-lovers with a baby?

Friends?

Where did that leave his new life? Would Madi move to his new job or would he move to Overlook? Would they co-parent from different states?

It all left a sour taste in his mouth.

Julian finished the shower after a few more passes over his cut, and dried off. He knotted the towel around his waist and wiped the condensation off the mirror.

One thing at a time, he thought.

He nodded to himself, rolled his shoulders back and looked into the mirror, fully expecting to see nothing but his tired eyes and stubble that needed to be shaved.

Instead what he saw made his blood run cold.

It was Madi. She was no longer in bed but standing beside it, facing the bedroom's main door. Both hands were clutched around her stomach. Even in profile Julian could see the sheer terror on her face.

Then she spoke.

It wasn't to him.

"Who are you?"

Chapter Ten

"You're going to tell me the truth or else," a man threatened. His voice was deep and raspy. Either from age or a hard-lived life. Julian couldn't get a visual on the man from his vantage point. All he could see was Madi slowly backing up.

"What truth?" Her words were hard but Julian could hear the undercurrent of fear.

He needed to take out the threat. He also needed to know if that threat had a gun pointed. Julian didn't want to rush out there only to have the unknown man fire off a few shots. There was a chance that he wouldn't be able to shield Madi in time. Or their unborn child.

Some risks were worth taking; that wasn't one of them.

"Loraine Wilson." His accent was odd. Off. If he was from the South, he was purposely hiding his drawl.

Julian quickly looked around the bathroom. He knew what it held—nothing that was equal to a gun. Julian grabbed his phone and fisted his hand. He'd just have to do it the old-fashioned way. Madi shook her head but stopped walking backward. To her absolute credit she kept her eyes everywhere but where he was.

"I didn't kill her," she said. "I don't know who did."

The man laughed.

It shot adrenaline through Julian's veins.

"Listen, if you want to make this hard from the start, I'm not one to argue, lady. Honestly? I like it when my prey has a little fight in them."

Julian flung the bathroom door open and threw his cell phone like a pro pitcher in dire need of a strikeout. The man, much too close to Madi, had not suspected anyone else was around. The surprise showed clear in his eyes right before the smartphone slammed into the side of his face. Something cracked. Julian didn't have time to figure out if it was his phone or the man's face. His focus had switched to the knife in the man's grip.

Rage pulsed through Julian.

Guns were easy. Knives took work. Knives combined with trying to get information? That ran right to torture.

Whoever he was, he would never be the same when Julian was through with him.

"Who the hell—" the man yelled, cradling his

face with one hand and trying to get his balance with the other.

Julian wasn't about to answer any questions. He used his considerable height to his advantage. With two powerful strides forward, he closed the distance between them and threw his foot out in a high kick. The man hadn't expected that, either. The kick landed square against his gut. He gasped and doubled over. It was a miracle that the man was able to put his knee down to retain some balance.

It was also a miracle Julian's towel stayed on.

The man wheezed, trying to get his breath back. It was too much of a break in Julian's opinion. He pulled back his fist, ready to deliver what he hoped would be a knockout blow when the tables were horribly turned.

What Julian had in height, muscle and power, the man had in speed. He maneuvered the knife around so quickly that all Julian could do was stumble back. Madi's scream heralded a hot, searing pain across his left side. He didn't have time to assess the damage. The man changed his momentum until it was on a backward arc headed for Julian's right side.

This time Julian was prepared.

He caught the man's wrist as the cool blade of the knife bit into his skin. It drew blood but wasn't as deep as the other had been.

And Julian didn't intend to let it go any deeper.

With his left hand wrapped around the man's wrist, Julian brought his right fist low. It hit the man's ribs. Hard.

But this man must have seen his fair share of fights.

He was quick on the uptake again. With his free hand he delivered a quick jab to the first wound he'd inflicted.

Julian couldn't help the grunt of pain. Or the vulnerability it created. The men detangled from each other. Julian took a breath, knowing every second was precious in a fight meant to have only one ending, when the lighting in the room changed.

Darkness was followed by something weirdly shaped coming right at them. Julian backpedaled. His opponent did not. The bedside lamp hit his face so hard that Julian almost felt the pain.

The man didn't yell out. He didn't even groan.

He just dropped like a sack of potatoes.

Julian lunged for the knife as soon as the man's fingers went limp around it. It was covered in blood. *His* blood. Yet Julian didn't care. All his focus swept up to the pregnant woman breathing heavily at his side.

Madi's eyes were wide, her cheeks flushed.

"You hit him," Julian said, awe in his voice.

Madi looked between him and the man on the floor.

"I did."

"With a lamp."

She nodded.

"It was either that or a pillow, and I didn't think that would be as effective."

Despite himself, Julian chuckled. The movement hurt. He looked down at the first cut he'd been given. It was deep. Not life-threatening, but it would need stitches. He pressed his hand against it. Madi gasped.

"Oh, Julian, you're hurt!"

"I'm fine," he said, fending her off. He put the knife on the bed and backtracked to the bathroom, eyes never leaving the man on the floor. He swiped the fresh pair of boxers and jeans he'd laid out before his shower and stepped into them in record time. Blood ran down to stain them before he could cover his wound again. There was no time to worry about it. "Do you have something I can restrain him with?" he asked, coming back and kneeling down next to the unconscious man's side. "You got him good with the lamp but I don't want to take any chances."

Madi thought for a moment and then snapped her fingers.

"I have a pair of handcuffs in my room. They're pink and fluffy but they'll do the trick." That got

Julian's attention. He quirked an eyebrow up. The color in her cheeks darkened. "They were a gag gift from one of my college girlfriends but they really do work."

She didn't say anything more and hurried out of the room. Julian leaned over the man and for the first time took a really good look at him.

He was clean-shaven, including the blond hair cut close to his scalp. Julian guessed he was around his age, maybe younger even. His relaxed face held a youthfulness, even if the rest of him looked on the worn side. Julian lifted up the bottom of his shirt, which had shifted open in the tussle. A tattoo of a scorpion was faded against his side. It looked familiar but Julian couldn't place it. Other than that there were no telling signs that pointed to who he was or why he was there.

Julian moved to the pockets of the man's slacks, marveling at how well dressed he was. It didn't fit with the way he had spoken. Or his knife. The man looked like he should be on Wall Street, not creeping around a bed-and-breakfast in Tennessee, threatening a pregnant innkeeper for information about a murder. Something was off. Something was *really* off.

There was nothing of importance in his right pocket. Lint and a stick of gum. No ID or cell phone. Julian moved to search the other.

That was when he heard it.

A creak. From the stairs. Short and whining but definitely there. Madi's room was down the hall, not on the first floor. There was no reason why she should have been there. Julian jumped up and hurried to the door. Adrenaline rushed back into his veins.

The second-floor landing was laid out with the stairs in the middle. A half wall surrounded them, keeping guests from falling on their way to the two guest suites. Julian was in the one closest to the opening of the stairs. Loraine and Nathan's room was to his right and behind the stairs. Madi's private quarters were in the corner, on the opposite side of him.

A more-than-troubling distance when that creak in the stairs turned into a mass of dark hair that in no way belonged to Madi. Julian silently cursed himself for leaving the knife on the bed but there was no time to retrieve it. Another stroke of bad luck in a long line of unfortunate events.

Madi walked out of her room holding fuzzy pink handcuffs, just as the new arrival made it out onto the landing. Like the unconscious man, this one also wore a nice shirt and slacks, as if he'd simply taken a wrong turn at a business convention and just so happened to find himself in a closed inn. Unlike the man Julian had fought before, this one didn't have a knife.

He had a gun.

SCREAMING WAS POINTLESS, and yet Madi did it anyway.

The man at the stairs didn't seem put off by the sound. In fact, he was smiling. Between that and the pistol in his hand, Madi felt like she had woken in a worse nightmare than before.

"Well, I can't say I've ever been greeted by *that* before." The man motioned to the handcuffs. "But I'm always up for new experiences."

Madi's blood ran cold. This time she couldn't play it cool. She couldn't keep eye contact, hoping to give Julian the element of surprise. This time she couldn't help but look for the dark-eyed man who had been her savior.

And there he was.

Standing in the doorway of the guest suite, staring right back at her.

"Madi, run!"

The man on the stairs followed her gaze just as Julian yelled. He cursed and turned his aim. Madi instantly thawed. A feeling of such possessive power overcame her, like it had with the lamp. With a wild war cry she threw the second thing that night.

The pink fuzzy handcuffs flew through the air. They hit the man's head, much like Julian's cell phone had. This one, however, was faster on the uptake. He managed to get a shot off before he stumbled.

Madi's heart almost stopped. Fear replaced any and all bravado she'd had. Julian had disappeared from view. Had he been hit?

"What the—"

The man moved around the half wall to get the same answer. Julian was polite enough to oblige.

He rammed into the intruder like a defensive back. The man shot again but the bullet whizzed over Julian and embedded itself into the doorjamb. This time Madi listened to Julian's original order.

She turned on her heel and retreated into her living space, holding her stomach as she went. She had been taught to stay and fight, but with her daughter along for the ride? Those stakes were too high.

Madi hurried around the room, searching it like she'd never once stepped foot inside. Adrenaline was making her movements jerky, her mind sluggish. She wanted to help but for the life of her couldn't think past the fuzzy pink handcuffs.

And she'd just thrown those.

A man groaned so loud Madi froze on spot. Another gunshot rang through her inn. Footsteps thundered across the hardwood. She clutched her stomach but it was Julian who ran into view.

"Bedroom," he yelled out, breathing labored.

Madi listened as Julian threw the door shut and locked it. He did the same in the bedroom the second he was through the door. Then he yanked over her dresser. It crashed to the floor and blocked most of the door.

"Any guns in here?" he asked, pulling her toward the window.

"No! The cops took my handgun!"

Julian cursed.

"We need to get out of here," he said, changing tactics. He nodded to the window. Madi understood. She just didn't like it. A crash vibrated through the floor. Madi unlocked the window and started to slide it up.

"There's nowhere to go, you hicks," the man yelled. The door handle shook. Then the door quaked. Next came a bullet. The mirror over the bed shattered but it did nothing to slow Julian's pace. He had Madi up and out of the window before half of the glass could even hit the floor. When he was at her side, he lowered his voice. It by no means undercut the severity of their situation. He grabbed her hand.

"I need you to guide us out of here, Madi."

They might have been standing on a roof at night, chased by a man with a gun, but feeling Julian's hand was like taking a deep, steadying breath.

She nodded.

"Let's go!"

Chapter Eleven

The roof was mostly flat outside Madi's bedroom and bathroom. It hung over the downstairs lounge before dropping off at the back patio. They could have run to the edge and jumped down right next to the back door but all she could think about was the drop. And how the gunman would have an easy sight line to their backs.

So she cut left and hurried along the second story until the flat roof ended and the one that pitched high over the kitchen rose above them.

"We could jump off here or climb over," Madi explained, already slightly out of breath. "There's another small overhang on the other side that has that big wooden trellis attached. I—I don't know if it can hold our weight, though. Just like I don't know if I can make the jump here."

The night sky was clear above them. It was the only reason the moon was giving off enough light that Madi could just make out Julian's expression. He was looking between her two options and, no doubt, playing through both scenarios in his head. Neither was ideal.

A gunshot tore through the quiet. Glass shattered. Madi squeezed Julian's hand like her life depended on it.

"Do you think you can climb this?"

"I've done it before, just not while I was pregnant," she admitted. "And not at night."

Clear as the day it wasn't. Julian's face hardened into worry. Their pursuer's voice, yelling something Madi couldn't make out, seemed to tip the scale of which option was more worth the risk. Julian let go of her hand and motioned to the field of shingles to their left.

"Ladies first."

Madi was proud of herself for several reasons as she placed her hands out and walk-climbed up the pitched roof. For one, after her shower she'd dressed in comfortable clothes instead of her pajamas, fully expecting to help the boys after she was rested. That meant she was rocking her most flexible pair of yoga pants and a loose blouse that didn't complain as she moved at the weird angle. She'd also fallen asleep with her tennis shoes on. Now they were a godsend, gripping the shingles with a proficiency her body naturally lacked thanks to the sheer awkwardness of almost being in her third trimester.

She was also pleased that despite the danger,

her nerves had gone weirdly calm. She focused on her hand and foot placement. Focused on the sound of Julian's breathing and movement behind her.

They needed to get as far away from the man as they could.

The ridge above the kitchen wasn't the highest point of the inn but it was tall enough to be of concern. With extreme caution, Madi and Julian crept to the other side, where they needed to climb down to where the roof flattened and ended with the overhang. Madi had half a mind to suggest they just hide on the roof.

Maybe their mystery man would think navigating a roof at night would be way too stupid for a pregnant woman and injured man to attempt. Maybe he'd think they had jumped and were currently fleeing.

Maybe—

Another shot rang out somewhere over their heads. It caught Madi so off guard she fell on her side in the middle of trying to take it slow down the side of the peak. Julian scrambled after her, grabbing at her shirt. He caught a handful of the fabric but couldn't stop the two of them from sliding down. Her on her side, Julian on his stomach. A scream caught in Madi's throat, fearing the worst as they skidded downward, when her feet stopped on flat ground. They'd made it to the overhang.

Julian cursed something awful as he let her go and caught the roof with his hands. Together they fumbled into easier positions. Then Julian was pulling her up and hurrying to the edge.

"We have to hurry."

Madi couldn't agree more.

She followed him to the edge and tried really hard not to think about their combined weights. The trellis was made of sturdy wood entwined with vines. It covered the entire left side of the kitchen wall from the ground to a few inches above the roofline. Madi turned around and accepted Julian's help in getting her first foothold.

She tried thinking light thoughts as her shoe slid into the second one. Then her hand into another.

For a moment they both waited for the terrifying crack of their only lifeline breaking.

Thankfully, and much to their surprise, it never happened.

"Hurry," Madi exclaimed.

Julian did as he was told.

Together, they awkwardly climbed down. Madi did so with less speed and much less grace. Her stomach was too big. Every movement she had to angle away from the makeshift ladder. She missed the last few gaps altogether because of it. She let out a small scream. Two strong hands caught her back and side before any damage could be done.

Then it was just the two of them on the ground.

Julian's head swiveled. Madi didn't have the patience. She started to run around the corner of the house but those strong hands held her firm.

"We don't know if there's more of them," he whispered, pulling her closer to his chest. "The house isn't safe for you."

Madi didn't like how he put emphasis on *for you*.

"Well, you're not going in there, either, then," she said, trying to stay as quiet. "If it's not safe for me then it's not safe for you." Every time she thought they had a moment of safety, something would burst that bubble. Now being on the ground was no exception. A man's voice let out a string of expletives somewhere across the roofline.

Julian took that as a reason to get moving. He pulled her along with him around the back of the house. A scuffle sounded on the roof near where they had been, proving his move to be a good one. Whoever their pursuer was, he was nothing if not determined.

A truly terrifying trait given the context.

They crept along the side of the inn, keeping close to the house until the back patio was only a few feet away. Madi didn't need lamplight to see the blood glistening on both of Julian's sides.

Nor the limp he'd adopted since their run across the roof.

Madi had fallen in love with Hidden Hills' off-the-beaten-path location, but at the moment, it felt like a point in the bad guys' column. How could they go up against a gun when Julian didn't even have shoes?

It wasn't a fair fight.

Madi fumbled for Julian's hand. She squeezed it as a thought zipped her spine straight.

What if they didn't need to fight at all?

"I know the forest like the back of my hand," Madi said with no segue. She looked over to the stone path that she'd walked less than two days ago with the guests and Jenna. "Get us to the tree line at the end of that path and I can make us disappear."

JULIAN STAYED AT Madi's back like the shield he was prepared to become if the gunman saw them make a break for the trees. She stumbled once but then, together, they fell into a groove.

They became a unit.

One that wasn't spotted.

Julian felt relief uncoil inside him less than a step inside the forest. He wanted to keep moving but Madi decreased her pace to an almost crawl.

"I—I need to slow down," she panted, hand

rubbing her stomach. "It's not good to—to push myself unless I have to."

Julian fought the urge to run back to the inn, find their mystery man and beat him to a pulp. How dare he or *anyone* threaten the well-being of his child? How dare they put Madi in this position?

Julian couldn't stop his anger from rolling into even angrier words. Madi patted his hand, meeting his eyes with a small smile.

"I'm okay," she whispered. "Just not used to all of this exertion. Usually getting out of the recliner is a chore."

He nodded that he understood and let her lead.

During his earlier stay at Hidden Hills, Madi and he had explored several of the nearby trails, but the more they walked, the farther off those trails Madi took them. Julian marveled that the woman could even see where she was going, let alone guide them to a strategic location. Yet he wasn't about to doubt her sure-footed movements. Not when most of his attention was behind them.

The two men had surprised him well enough. Julian wasn't about to give a third the satisfaction.

Madi slowed as the ground started to slope downward. The trees thinned out. Julian's eyes made the adjustment for the change in the light. At least here he could see farther than a foot in front of him. The sound of running water became more pronounced until finally Madi stopped.

"Do you think he's following us?" Her question was so soft. Vulnerable. In the new light Julian could see her exhaustion in more detail. Her shoulders sagged; her back hunched slightly. Her lips were thinned and pulled down in a frown that was equal parts thought and worry.

"He may be trying," Julian said, "but I don't think he realized we ran off into the woods in the first place. And if he did, I don't think even I could have tracked us here. You did one hell of a job of getting us lost."

That frown rocked up into the smallest of smiles.

"The perk of growing up in a smaller than small town." She motioned behind her. "There's not much to do other than explore."

The water belonged to a small creek. They walked to its edge. Julian dipped his foot in. It was cold.

"If we follow this it will either take us to my closest neighbor—" she pointed to the west and then pointed to the east "—or the county road, where we may or may not be able to flag someone down."

"And how far are we talking to each location?"

Madi bit her lip. Julian pretended it didn't distract him just a bit.

"I'd say to the Jansens' place it's…maybe two miles? The county road maybe a bit less than that but the trek there is a little rockier than here."

Julian pulled his hand away from the bigger of the two wounds on his side and surveyed the cut, trying to think strategically about which direction to go. The bleeding had slowed. He made sure to keep his wince internal. Madi's eyes were already wide enough as she took in the wound.

"Here, try this." Madi grabbed the bottom of her shirt. She tore it but instead of it going along the bottom, it ripped up over her stomach. "Well, crap. I was trying to be cool. They always make it look so easy in movies." Julian chuckled. Madi moved closer. "Go ahead and tear off a piece if you can. The shirt's already ruined."

He did as he was told, grabbing one side and making a smaller, more precise tear. His knuckles brushed against the skin of her stomach in the process. She tensed. Julian took the piece of cloth and pressed it to his cut. He didn't move away. Neither did Madi.

Slowly she angled her chin up, meeting his eye.

"After I found out I was pregnant, a part of me didn't want you to answer when I called." Her voice was soft, low. "After what happened when I was a kid… Well, the unknown can be insanely terrifying for me. I was worried that if you answered and I told you, you wouldn't want to have anything to do with us, with me. But truthfully, I think I was more afraid that you would." She put her hand on his bare chest. The warmth in that touch reached every part of him. "No matter what happens later, I have to tell you—right *now*—I'm really glad you're here."

Madi pushed up on her tiptoes.

Her lips were soft. Oh so soft.

He could have stayed against them forever.

But then she ended the kiss as quickly as it had started.

She took a step back, giving him space, and let her hand fall from his chest.

Julian knew that now wasn't the time to talk about what they meant to each other, what priorities the child between them would shift and change, and how their choices would affect their futures. He knew their current focus should be on getting out of the woods and away from the men who were after Madi. He couldn't afford being distracted. Not when Madi's and their daughter's lives were on the line. Yet looking at her staring back at him expectantly, lips as beautiful as the rest of her, Julian almost caved.

Almost.

"I think our best bet would be to go to the neighbors'," he said after clearing his throat. "They should at least have a phone or car we could use."

It might have been a trick of the light but Julian

thought he saw a brief look of hurt pass across Madi's face. One second it was there; the next she was nodding.

"I'm right behind you."

Chapter Twelve

Two miles might as well have been ten. Madi's swollen ankles and general exhaustion sank in twenty minutes into their trek following the creek.

"I need to rest," she finally admitted. "And I need to do it now."

Julian didn't complain. He hovered around her with concern, his movements quick and rigid. Together they eased her to the ground between two trees while she tried not to focus on the pain radiating up her legs.

"These tennis shoes were made for walking but the pregnant belly, lack of sleep and ravenous hunger were not."

She tried her darnedest to give him a reassuring smile. It must have fallen flat instead. He crouched down next to her, hand already trying to steady her as she readjusted to get comfortable. Or at least to get to some semblance of it.

"I just need to rest," she said. "That's it."

"You need to not be in these woods in the first place," he growled back.

Madi put her hand over his. Julian's anger was touching.

"I won't argue with you there. I'd much rather be back in bed. Blissfully asleep until my bladder punched me awake." She sighed. "Which, if I were more hydrated, would be an issue." As it was, Madi was more concerned with keeping off her feet. Their jaunt through the woods hadn't been so daunting until the adrenaline had fully worn off. Thankfully that meant the mystery men weren't with them. In fact, Madi was positive they hadn't followed. The sounds that had filled the world around them for the last twenty minutes or so had belonged to insects, the wind and animals that were between curiosity and sleep.

"I should have grabbed my phone," he added, still grounded in his anger. "After I threw it back in the room. I should have grabbed it."

"Cell phone service out here is spotty at best. Even if you had, I don't think it would have helped."

"It wouldn't have hurt."

Madi shrugged. "Honestly, I'm still impressed you used it as a weapon. Wearing nothing but a towel. I mean, it's no set of fuzzy pink handcuffs, but it was still impressive."

"I may not know what's going on here, but if

there's anything I've learned tonight it's that our kid is going to have one hell of a throwing arm." She couldn't see it, but Madi heard the faint smile in his voice.

It made her chest squeeze. She rubbed her stomach and smiled.

"There are worse things we could hand down."

Julian shifted but didn't stand. The cloth beneath his hand had changed colors completely now. In the dark it was easy to forget he was hurt. Who were these men? Who sent them? She was so focused on those questions, she'd forgotten to be vigilant about checking up on Julian. A flood of shame rushed through her. Julian might have been her savior but that didn't mean he was immune to danger.

"You need to get help," Madi decided. "Keep following the creek and you'll run straight into the Jansens' house. You won't be able to miss it. They're friendly enough, though I imagine Bill might have some questions before he extends any offers."

"I'm not leaving you, Madi."

"You're hurt. I'm only tired. There's a big difference there."

Julian shook his head.

"We got lucky tonight. I don't want to test how much luck we have left. Just because those men aren't here now doesn't mean they won't get here eventually," he said. "I'll be damned if I leave you to face them alone." He took a breath. When he spoke again there was a new emotion behind his words. One Madi hadn't yet heard from the man. "When the first man saw you while I was in the bathroom, did he look surprised at all?"

Madi felt her skin start to crawl again. The shower had woken her up. She'd assumed it was Julian. Her thoughts had tangled together, wondering what would happen when he was done—would she offer to let him sleep with her? The couch was so small that he'd never fit. Then another, hotter what-if had sprung up. It had been enough to get her out of bed and send her in search of water. Though she never made it past the getting-out-of-bed part. When the man had walked into view, he'd been smiling.

"No," she answered. "Not even a little."

"Which means those men came in with knives and guns, ready to *use* them, already knowing you were pregnant."

It was a sobering thought. Suddenly, Madi felt more tired.

"I can hide," she offered, still unmoved from her original plea. "Long enough for you to go get help and come back. I know these woods. I know what to listen for." Madi angled her face to see him better. The moonlight through the shadows of the trees illuminated only the tilt of his head and his brows drawn in together. "Julian, you're no good to me—to us—if you lose your health, and I'm here to tell you, I need to get off my feet for a good bit."

Julian wavered. She could feel it through his hand still on her arm, still trying to make sure she was steady sitting there. No part of him wanted to go, yet his mind was coming to the same conclusion hers had already. She wasn't going to be walking anytime soon, he was still bleeding, and if by some chance the men did find the two of them the outcome wouldn't be favorable. Definitely not for Julian. And if something happened to him? Madi would have no hope.

"I don't like this," Julian finally said, voice thrumming low.

"And I can't make the walk right now. This is our best option."

He cursed low but stood tall.

"We're going to make you a damned good hiding place first."

For a man who had once told her he'd grown up in a big city, Julian was decidedly handy when it came to camouflaging a rather large woman in the woods at night. Where there had been hesitation before, there was now dedication. He pulled her deeper into the trees and spent several minutes rearranging the foliage, creating a wall with part of a fallen tree and branches he'd collected.

He pulled back and stalked around her. He made a few adjustments until he was satisfied.

"I don't like this," he repeated afterward. "But I think even if the sun comes up, you'd be hard to find here."

"I'd have to agree."

The truth was, Madi could barely see a thing around her. She felt like she was in a tree without the hassle of climbing it.

Julian lowered himself to a crouch. Madi wished she could reach out and touch him. To give him another kiss. One that showed more than her appreciation. One that showed that her desires ran much deeper. But that would defeat the purpose. Julian wouldn't leave then, even when the blood running from his wounds would only continue to run.

Instead Madi took a deep breath.

"Be careful, Julian."

His words were grit in the dark.

"I'll be back before you know it."

THE JANSENS WEREN'T HOME, but that didn't stop Julian. He tried the front and back doors. Both were locked. Same for the first-floor windows. His patience didn't extend past that.

"I owe you one, Bill."

Julian shattered the window that took up the top half of the back door and tossed the rock he'd used into the bushes. He snaked his arm through and easily unlocked the dead bolt.

The Jansens' home was filled with cool air and silence. Julian would have preferred to find someone home, even if he'd have to explain himself in record time, but he was sure no one had stirred because of his break-in. At least now he could search for a landline without worry of being arrested.

He moved with purpose through the first floor, turning on lights as he went. He thrummed with the urgency of Madi out in those woods. He didn't need stealth right now. He needed speed. The living room, dining room and kitchen were well lived-in, but no phone or computer was in sight. Julian had never had a strong opinion about the current state of technology, but in that moment, he loathed cell phones.

Surely a house out in the middle of nowhere would invest in *one* landline?

He moved upstairs, all thoughts of being considerate thrown out the window. He knew he was trailing blood from his bare feet. He knew the doorknobs he touched were graced with a crimson coat. He knew that anyone from outside the situation would view him as a madman.

Just as Julian knew that every moment he was in the house, Madi was in the woods. There wasn't time to waste.

The two bedrooms upstairs weren't empty but

they had no phones, either. Not even the room that seemed to be used as a library.

Julian couldn't help the frustration that kicked in at the sight of the empty desktop next to the window. Who were these people and how did they communicate with the outside world? Did they use powerful walkie-talkies to stay connected? Morse code? Signal fires?

He grabbed a loose piece of paper, intending to throw *something* to feel an ounce of control, when a light in the distance caught his eye.

Hope sprang eternal. On the opposite side of where he'd come out of the woods was a structure tucked back in the trees. It was small, but there was an undeniable glow at the windows.

That was all Julian needed.

He left the house and struck out across the clearing and into the trees. There was a dirt path leading to the small building but branches and roots littered the way. The path wasn't well-used; neither was the building.

The wood and siding were fading and chipped. A rusted-out wheelbarrow sat beneath a boarded-up window while an assortment of gardening tools cluttered the perimeter. The building was either a roomy shed or a small mother-in-law suite. Julian hoped for the latter. Surely it would have a phone. If it didn't, then he hoped the place was used for storage. Including an ATV or motorized bike of some sort. Anything to help Madi out of the woods without adding more stress to her body.

Julian moved closer to the main door but paused at the second window. It was only partially boarded up, light from inside pouring out.

Adrenaline shot into Julian's already-exhausted bloodstream.

"No," he whispered, hoping his eyes were playing tricks on him. Yet the longer he stared, nothing changed. "No, no, no."

He moved over a few feet and liberated a broken hoe from the discarded items spread out next to the building. The handle was snapped in half but he could still do some damage with it if needed.

Julian squared his shoulders and went to the door. He took a deep breath and tried the handle.

It was locked.

"I owe you again, Bill."

This time Julian didn't break a window.

Instead he kicked down the door.

Inside sure wasn't a mother-in-law suite.

The space was mostly open. A few boxes covered in dirt and dust took up places across the faded floor. Two folding chairs stood against the back wall, an old milk crate flipped over between them. The overhead light reached every part of the room, but there was a flashlight on one of the chairs. It was turned off but pointing at the only real thing of note in the building.

A man bound to a metal chair, surrounded by blood. He was hunched over, completely still.

Julian hurried over, keeping his sight line to the only open door, and immediately went for the man's neck. Again he didn't stir but then, slowly, the beat of a pulse pressed against Julian's fingers.

It was a welcome feeling, though it didn't last long. Julian cussed and then said the second thing that came to mind.

"What's going *on* in this town?"

Chapter Thirteen

Madi was trying not to fall asleep, so she gave herself permission to think about the first time she and Julian had made love.

It was the last day of his stay at Hidden Hills and Madi had agreed, once again, to have drinks with him after dinner. They'd already spent the day before together, drinking sweet tea outside until the late hours of the night. They'd talked, laughed and explored the property. Neither had seemed keen on leaving the other's company.

Their time together went outside the bounds of her duties as an innkeeper but Madi couldn't get the man out of her thoughts.

She couldn't stop how she felt, either.

Being around Julian had infused her with a giddiness that made her feel carefree, wistful and capable of anything, all at once. A schoolgirl crush amplified by a shrinking timeline.

Then, right before dinner, Julian had shown up at her door. Dressed down, up or anything in between, Julian Mercer looked good. Madi's brain could no more deny that fact than her body could ignore it.

And that night, Madi had all but sighed as he stood in the doorway smiling.

"I was getting restless in my room, so thought I'd swing by and see if you wanted to join me on a little walk before dinner."

It had been a smooth line in a smooth voice.

Madi had grinned wide.

"Already restless, huh? Don't worry, I can get you checked out of here as early as you want tomorrow. I happen to know the owner."

She'd winked, trying her best at transferring that feeling of being carefree into flirting, but Julian's smile had wavered somewhat.

"As much as I appreciate the connection, I believe feeling restless has more to do with wanting to spend time with the owner, not leaving." Madi could still remember the heat that had crawled up her neck. Not because his words had caught her off guard, but because she'd felt the same.

"I've never made someone feel restless before," she had responded, not trying to hide the blush that had conquered her cheeks.

Julian had taken a small step forward. Madi hadn't moved an inch.

"I think you're underestimating yourself."

He'd reached out and brushed his fingers across

her cheek. He'd gone through the motions of tucking a strand of hair behind her ear. When his objective was complete he was back on the other side of the door frame, holding his arm out to her.

Madi's body had revved at the contact, just as her chest had fluttered at the closeness. It had all made her terribly impulsive.

"I'd like to change if that's all right," she'd said. "Would you like to come in and wait?"

"It wouldn't bother me in the slightest."

He'd followed her into the living area but stayed at the couch. Madi's heart had raced as she'd gone through her bedroom, looking for an outfit that would do her justice. She'd settled on a dress that wasn't formal, wasn't casual and made her legs look absolutely wonderful.

The only catch?

"Um, Julian?" The man was at the door in a second. "Could you pull this up for me? I can't reach the zipper."

Later, Madi would wonder if she'd unconsciously picked that dress so that Julian would need to help her with it. That he'd have to run his hand up her bare back. So she'd have to feel the heat of his skin so close to hers.

Sitting in the dark, back against a tree and hand protectively on her stomach, Madi still didn't know.

"There," Julian had said when the zipper had

reached the top. Madi had turned around, ready to thank him, but any and all words had stalled on her tongue. Dark eyes had locked onto hers with a look that Madi didn't need help translating. "Perfect," he'd breathed. "Just perfect."

It had been a movie kiss. Unexpected, completely wanted. Hard, searching. Filled with heat that traveled with every swipe of their tongues and every gliding touch across their skin.

What had started as a mostly innocent task had boiled over into longing that had somehow formed between relative strangers in less than two days.

Every moment was so right. When Julian undid his handiwork and helped the dress hit the floor, hands and fingers skating along her skin. When Madi lifted his shirt to feel the hardness of his chest and abs without a barrier between them before moving down to ease the rest of his clothes off. When Julian looped his finger in her panties and pulled them down to join their other clothes on the floor. When he hoisted her naked body up into his arms and took her to the bed, not once breaking their kiss. When he pushed inside her and she yelled out in pleasure.

It all had felt right. From the top of her hair to the end of her toes, moving with and against Julian felt unbelievably amazing.

And then he'd stayed at the inn for a week. Madi had never been happier.

But then the real world had come knocking. Julian was supposed to leave for his interview. The one that would lead him to his new life. A life she wouldn't fit into. Hidden Hills, Overlook… They were her life. Julian deserved to have his own.

So Madi had called it off before it ever really started.

Look what good that had done.

Julian was tangled in the same dangerous web Madi had found herself caught in. He'd committed a crime to try to protect her and had gotten hurt. Never mind the "hey, I'm pregnant and she's yours," which must have thrown him for a loop.

Madi had always tried to be a good person, better with each passing day…and yet…bad seemed to follow her.

She sighed into the chill that had started to make her shiver. Her focus needed to be on the present, not the past. Not the future. Someone had killed one of her guests. A detective had been kidnapped, a coroner had been killed and two men had come for her with weapons ready.

Why?

It was a question that stayed with her as the darkness around her started to lighten. Minutes had become what felt like hours. Through the treetops, the sky glowed a soft orange and yellow, tinged with strips of pink. A sense of dread weighted Madi's heart at the sight. It was time to go.

Her feet and legs protested when she finally managed to stand. She braced herself as her head swam for a moment.

"This is going to be a long day," she muttered to the tree that had been her backboard. "I'm already starving."

Julian had been right. Her hiding place would have continued to do its job during the daytime. It felt like she was in some kind of wild jungle, trying to find a hidden waterfall or temple.

"And I have to pee something fierce," she continued, moving branches around her out of the way, careful not to lose her balance. "My luck, though? The cavalry would show up while I was in the middle of relieving my poor, abused bladder. Yep. That's definitely how good my luck has been lately. Miller would probably be the one to do it, too. Ugh, with a camera crew to boot. National, not just local."

The trees around her kept quiet as she mumbled out more complaints. Then, finally, she saw the water. It didn't help her bladder situation but it somehow made her feel more calm. She knew where she was and how to get to where she needed to be. Still, she stretched wide and was about to grumble some more in an attempt for catharsis when the sound of an engine echoed up the creek.

Madi slunk back against the closest tree.

The creek was too small for a boat and the creek bed was too narrow for a car. Her heartbeat sped up as she waited.

Then one heck of a sight came into view.

It was Julian.

On a riding lawn mower.

Madi stepped out of her hiding place. A feeling of such acute relief replaced every other thought in her head. Her hormones took the already-intense emotion and tripled it. When Julian cut the engine a few feet from her, Madi felt the tears in her eyes.

"Are you okay?" He jumped from the worn seat and was at her side in a flash. His hands wrapped around her arms. Always trying to steady her.

Madi nodded.

"I—I'm just glad you're okay. I was worried."

Julian's expression softened. But only for a moment. Madi realized then that there were two bandages over his knife wounds, both taped to his bare skin. He also had on work boots.

He caught her eye.

"I would have been here a lot sooner but… Well, let's just say you're not going to believe what happened. I barely do."

THE HOSPITAL'S FLUORESCENTS weren't helping his mood. Nor was the angry man in front of him. Julian rubbed at his temples. A tension headache was on the long list of things currently plaguing him. The top of that list was red faced and tapping his badge.

"I've been doing this job a long time," Detective Miller said. "A long time. Do you know how many ridiculous excuses and stories I've heard through the years?"

"I'm sure plenty," Julian answered, knowing it had been rhetorical. His patience with the lawman was thinning. "But that doesn't mean a thing when it comes to what happened last night. What's been happening the last two days. Someone tried to frame Madi. They tried to hurt her. And, for whatever reason, that extended to Detective Holloway."

Miller's lips thinned. The crease in his forehead deepened as he became even more unhappy, if such a thing were possible.

"The man you just happened to find," Miller stated. Again.

Julian took a deep breath. He reminded himself that picking up the smaller man and throwing him across the room would do nothing to help his case. It certainly wouldn't help Madi. She'd already been through enough without adding fuel to Miller's fire.

"Listen, I know you have issues with Madi and the rest of her family." Julian readjusted his tone. He wanted to get out of the lobby's corner where they'd been talking since the detective had arrived. Pushing the man's buttons by adopting an even angrier attitude, no matter how badly he wanted to, would only delay him reuniting with Madi. Not to mention giving an even bigger lead to her attackers. "If it was anyone else, you'd already be out there looking for the couple who shot your colleague in the hand and the men who had no problem trying to torture and kill a pregnant woman." The detective's jaw visibly hardened but he let Julian continue. "You were with us when the coroner's van was attacked. You saw the damage at the inn. Holloway told you himself that he'd never seen Madi or me before. Just because this isn't all adding up doesn't mean Madi is to blame. And you know it. So, please, let me take her to the ranch so she can get some rest. She and the baby need it."

Miller's stare was unwavering. To Julian's surprise, he didn't spout any hotheaded rebuttal. Instead he sucked on his teeth, then came to a decision. Julian just hoped it was the right one.

"You're tying your ship to hers. If she goes down, you will, too. I hope you realize that."

Julian nodded. Miller looked over as Detective Devereux walked in from the hallway. Desmond was at his side.

"Don't leave town," he said, giving his badge one more tap. "And, Mr. Mercer, just because

Madeline isn't behind everything that's happening doesn't mean she isn't in the center of it. If I were you, I'd watch out."

Julian didn't respond. Not that Miller expected it. He gave Desmond no more than a stiff nod of acknowledgment before leaving the hospital with his colleague. Julian met the Nash triplet with a less-than-enthused nod himself.

"I still think it's a huge conflict of interest having Miller run this case," he greeted. "He clearly is partial as hell when it comes to the lot of you."

"As much as I'd agree with you in any other instance, I will say that for once, Detective Miller's anger issues might work in our favor." Julian raised his eyebrow at that. Desmond explained, "He'll try his hardest to find a way to pin this on us. Now that this case has picked up attention and involved another officer, Miller will need hard evidence to make that happen."

"And since Madi isn't some deranged puppet master behind all this pulling the strings—"

"He'll find the real puppet masters," Desmond finished.

Julian saw the logic there, but that didn't mean he had to like it. He squared his shoulders. The need to protect Madi was ringing through him once again.

"Not unless I find them first."

IT HAD BEEN a long while since Madi had been in bed with Julian and yet, hours after she had thought about their first time, there they were… in bed together again.

This time there was a lot more between them. Not just physically. Lying on her side, facing him, Madi ran a hand over her stomach beneath the covers and met his eyes with a sigh.

"I'm fine," she reiterated. "We're both fine. The doctor checked us out. All he said was to get some rest and drink some water. And definitely don't go climbing over the roof again."

Madi gave a wry smile. He returned it, though there was still undeniable concern in his stare.

"When we get to more solid ground on this whole thing, I'd like to know more." His smile turned sweet, quiet but heartfelt. "About the pregnancy, about the baby. I have to admit, I don't know much about either in general."

Madi's heart squeezed. In a perfect world he would have gone along with her every step of the way after finding out they were pregnant. But she'd messed up that perfect world when she'd turned him away. Talking with him about the child they'd made was a painful reminder about what she'd rejected.

"I'd be happy to," she said honestly.

He nodded, his head against the pillow.

They were back at Des's house in Madi's old room. This time there was no wondering where Julian was or would be. After they'd eaten, Madi had made it clear she didn't want to be alone for the sleep they both needed to get. Julian had made it clear he was on the same page. He wasn't leaving Madi's side anytime soon.

"Is there anything I need to know now? Anything I should, uh, look out for?" Madi chuckled. It rubbed off on him. "What can I say? I'm so out of my element that I don't even know what to ask about specifically. Dilation? Sonogram? Applying for preschool early? Am I somewhere in the ballpark?"

Madi was beside herself with laughter.

"You're at least in the parking lot," she said when she could manage.

Julian grinned.

"Good."

"But all you need to know right now? Honestly, I'm about to pass out. I'm so tired. I mean, I'm always tired lately, but if I fall asleep in the middle of us talking, I'm sorry…and then *when*—not if—I wake up to pee for the billionth time, I apologize again." She reached out for his hand but hesitated. "She usually starts moving around when I first lie down. Want to see if you can feel her?"

Julian's entire demeanor changed. Madi worried she'd crossed some kind of line. But then, slowly, he reached out and met her hand in the middle. Madi shifted the blanket and guided him to her stomach. She lifted her shirt so he had the best chance of catching the little gymnast. His skin was, as always, so wonderfully warm.

It was comforting. So much so that she yawned.

"Don't worry if you can't feel her," she said, stifling a second one. "So far I'm the only one to catch her in the act."

Julian nodded stiffly. He was concentrating. It would have melted a part of Madi's heart had her eyelids not gotten so heavy.

He was just so warm.

Chapter Fourteen

Two days passed before Madi felt much more like herself. Not only had she slept through both nights, she'd taken several daytime naps. A feat that was harder than normal considering Julian hadn't left her side. Sure, he gave her space when they were in the house when she wanted it, but if she needed him he was there with seconds to spare.

His brow would pull in, he'd look at her stomach, and then he'd look into her eyes and she knew in her bones he was prepared for anything. Their close call at the inn had changed something between them. It was one thing to lie for her; it was another to see her and their child in danger.

Madi knew this because seeing him get stabbed, twice, had been so close to soul crushing that, even safe on the ranch, she worried about him, too. Especially since no one knew anything about those men, the couple who had taken Detective Holloway or who had killed Loraine.

The mysteries were slowly driving the Nash family crazy, Madi included. Now that she was back to normal she didn't like the idea of sitting on her hands any longer. A point she brought up at breakfast. Moments before it was shot down hard by Caleb and Des.

"This is the safest place you can be right now," Des said, frowning and shaking his head. "We can control what goes on here. Once you leave through the front gate it gets harder."

Caleb agreed, his cowboy hat bouncing as he nodded with enthusiasm.

"The department and Kilwin PD are more invested than ever in catching these people," he added. "They're following several leads. It's just taking some time. Don't make it more complicated for them by making yourself accidental bait."

Madi couldn't help it. She went for a section of her hair, ready to start an angry braid, but Julian caught her hand before she could clear the table. Neither Nash brother saw the action. Caleb and Des had never been the overbearing and aggressive type of brothers who hovered around the men she dated, but she had been surprised that neither had questioned Julian yet. Everyone was now on the same page about him being the father. She had expected the news to carry consequences for the burly man holding her hand against his thigh, trying to calm her down. Yet as far as she knew, none of the Nash brothers had flexed their sibling muscles at him.

Madi assumed their focus was elsewhere, and maybe at some point they'd start questioning his absence. Then again, she hadn't missed the embraces they'd each given Julian in the hospital after Madi and the baby had been cleared. They respected him.

"How about instead of town you can show me around the ranch?" he offered, speaking to her but addressing the table as a whole. "I've still only been here and the main house. I'd love to see the rest."

Des and Caleb shared a look. They didn't flat out say no but Madi recognized their "how do we say no without seeming like jerks" expressions. She'd been on the receiving end of them a few times during their angsty teenage years.

"May I point out that there's a patrol car at the gate, Deputy Hudson keeps driving through every few hours, *all* of the staff is on the lookout *and* my escort is an ex-marine who is built like a sexy, jacked-up house?" She held up her hand to keep them quiet so she could finish. "The same sexy, jacked-up house who went head-to-head with two armed men with nothing more than a cell phone and his fists. And, by the way, managed to get a big ole pregnant woman across a roof, down to the ground and to safety without a scratch. All while *he* was hurt."

Madi gave her brothers a pointed stare, nearly begging them to fight her. They shared another look. Julian squeezed her hand twice. She glanced over. His expression was blank. Or almost blank. Madi could have sworn there was a smile trying its darnedest to pull up those delicious lips.

Des was the first to concede. Caleb sighed for effect.

"Just don't do any of the trails," Des said. His face softened. "Please. You know how easy it is to be caught by surprise on one."

Madi's momentary frustration at her brothers disappeared. She looked between them and, as it happened sometimes, she saw the eight-year-old boys she'd sneaked off into the woods with for an innocent game of hide-and-seek. Another unspoken conversation occurred among the three of them. Madi couldn't explain it any more than she could ignore it.

"I won't take any unnecessary chances," she finally promised. "But I can't stay locked up in here forever, either."

"Okay," they said together.

"Make sure your phones are charged," Des added, standing with his empty plate. He scooped up Julian's and Madi's before shoulder checking

Caleb. He rolled his eyes and started collecting their empty cups and mugs.

Madi felt a twinge of excitement. She hadn't lied when she said Hidden Hills felt like home, but she couldn't deny she now felt ready to see how Julian liked the place where she'd grown up.

"I have to pee again but then I'll be ready to go," she said to him.

It earned a laugh. She beat him to the reason behind it. "And yes, I did have to go before I sat down for breakfast. Like I said, this girl loves Riverdancing on my bladder."

Julian gave her a little push up and then she was off. When she finished in the bathroom she pulled her phone off the charger with more pep in her step than she'd had in a while. Her phone had finally been returned the day before by Detective Devereux. They hadn't seen Miller since the hospital, which was A-OK with Madi.

The temperature outside wasn't too hot or too humid. Still, as soon as they got into his SUV Madi flipped on the AC.

"I thought we could park at the stables and walk around from there. I can show you the retreat, too. It's a quick walk from there."

Julian adjusted his shirt over the back of something in the waist of his jeans. He caught Madi's quizzical stare.

"Your brothers gave me a gun."

"They what?"

Julian shrugged.

"Honestly, I was expecting a stern talking-to so I'm okay with the gun." He smirked. "Still, it wasn't the weirdest thing that happened today."

Madi felt her eyebrow rise.

"What's weirder than my brothers slipping you a gun in the kitchen?"

He put the vehicle in Reverse and then pulled out onto the main road that ran through the ranch.

"I'd have to say it was being described as a, and I quote, 'sexy, jacked-up house.'" Madi's cheeks flamed to life. Julian laughed. "I mean, don't get me wrong, this sexy house is flattered. It just was a first for me."

Madi groaned.

"It's these darn hormones," she defended. "They killed the filter that usually keeps these things in my head!"

"But you still think I'm sexy, right?"

Julian actually winked.

It did a number on those same hormones that had already bypassed her personal filter. Heat of a different nature started to spread through her. When she answered, her voice had dipped lower. She motioned to her stomach.

"Clearly."

Julian didn't respond beyond the grin he was already wearing but when they parked outside the stables, the air around them had changed. Madi didn't know how to deal with it. She'd gone from offhandedly calling him sexy to wanting to take him to the back seat and show him just how bendy she still could be.

Hormones. It's the pregnancy hormones, she thought. *You also thought a bag of Cheetos was the best thing in the world last night.*

Yet Madi knew her lame excuse wasn't the entire truth.

She didn't think she had ever stopped wanting Julian.

He cut the engine, got out and walked around to her door. When he opened it, Madi felt like she was on fire. She bit her lip to stop herself from blurting something more dangerous than a weird compliment.

Julian reached out. She assumed it would be for her hand; instead, his knuckles brushed across her cheek.

"You are the sexiest of us all, Madi Nash."

His thumb hooked beneath the line of her jaw, sliding along it until he had her chin in his hand. She let him tilt her head up. He bent over to complete the advance.

Like she had done to him in the woods, Julian gave her a kiss that was soft and brief. Unlike their time in the woods, they weren't in immediate danger. They could do more if they wanted.

Did she—

Yes. Before she could even finish the thought she knew, without a doubt, she wanted to be taken by Julian. Again and again.

The real question was, did he want her? After all of this time? After everything that had already happened?

Someone cleared their throat. Julian was in front of her in a flash, eyes darting to the culprit.

"Ray!"

Ray Cutler gave an awkward little wave and smiled.

"Sorry, I didn't mean to interrupt." He pointed back to the stables behind him. The main doors were open, letting the breeze carry in front of the stalls. "I just got back from a ride with Clive."

Madi stumbled out of her seat and hoped her cheeks weren't as red as she assumed they were.

"That's awesome! I didn't know you knew how to ride."

Ray ran a hand through his hair and gave a hearty laugh.

"I'm not a pro or anything but I can get from point A to B without falling. Half the time at least." He walked over and outstretched his hand. Madi noted that along with a cowboy hat, he was wearing riding gloves and boots. It made him look at home. Madi was glad for it.

After the two mystery men had shown up at

the inn, they'd asked Ray to stay at the Wild Iris Retreat instead of returning to Hidden Hills. It looked like he was enjoying the ranch. It eased a little of the guilt that had been weighing on her since Loraine's body had been found.

Hidden Hills offered relaxation and beauty. Instead, both had been violently destroyed.

"I'm Ray," he introduced. Julian returned the shake.

"Julian."

"So I've heard." Ray stepped back and gave a sheepish look. "I may not be from around here but word travels fast. Your heroics this week have been sweeping through town. Here, too." He thumbed back to the barn, most likely referring to Clive, a family friend as well as the stable master. Also a lousy gossip if he was in a good mood.

"I wouldn't call what I did heroic," Julian responded. He gave Madi a quick look. "Just necessary."

That heat beneath Madi's skin burned even hotter. Apparently her hormones didn't care that Ray was there. Her body wanted Julian. Badly.

"Whatever you want to call it, it's a good thing you were around." Ray changed his attention to Madi. He cleared his throat before continuing. "I'm glad I ran into you. I wanted to apologize for telling the cops what I heard you say about Loraine. I knew it was just said in frustration and I didn't for a minute think you did it, but I didn't want to lie, either."

Madi waved her hand through the air, dismissing the thought.

"I wouldn't have wanted you to lie. You did the right thing. No worries here."

A small voice in the back of her head reminded Madi that the man next to her *had* lied. What would have happened if he hadn't?

"I'm just glad it didn't get you into any permanent trouble." He flashed another quick smile and then tipped his hat down. It looked like such a natural motion. One that the Nash men did like it was second nature. Either Ray had lived a life out on the land like they had on the ranch or he was a quick study. Whichever, the mantle of cowboy suited him. Though Madi's brothers would never let their prized hats get as dirty as the one Ray had on. A few black smudges showed along the side. Ray caught her eye. He chuckled. "Not all of us can be perfect, can we?"

A memory started to stir at his words. One that came with a gut punch of urgency. It must have shown on her face.

"You okay, Madi?" Julian asked, hand pressing on the small of her back. Ray's eyes had gone wide in alarm, as well. Madi tried to laugh off both of their concerns.

"Just a little spacey is all." She pointed to her

stomach. "This one has a way of making me a bit ditzy from time to time. Nothing to worry about. Just lost my words."

Ray kept searching her expression with concern, but Madi was starting to get tired of all the men giving her that look. She mustered up the best customer service smile she could and let it shine wholly on the man.

"I'm glad you're enjoying yourself, Ray. Please let any of us know if you need anything and we'll make it happen."

It did the trick. He loosened and nodded to them both again, heading to his cabin after they said goodbye.

"A bit ditzy?" Julian repeated, voice low. "Are you sure you're okay?"

"Have you ever had a word on the tip of your tongue, but for the life of you, you can't remember it?" Julian nodded. "All of a sudden it's like I need to remember that word but can't."

Julian's hand moved across her back so slowly that goose bumps spread across her skin.

"Then why don't we get your mind on something else so your subconscious can figure it out?"

Madi raised her eyebrow at that.

"Are you saying that you want to distract me, Mr. Mercer?"

Julian was smirking.

"I sure would like to try."

Chapter Fifteen

Madi might have had some trouble getting up from the occasional chair or low surface, but by God, she shimmied out of her shirt and threw it across the room like she had superpowers. Julian barely had time to shut and lock the barn's second-floor loft door. Then all he could do was take a moment to stare. It caught the woman off guard; her face turned a darker shade of red.

"O-oh no," she stammered. "Is this not what you meant when you said distraction?"

Julian answered by pulling his own shirt off. He threw it away with a smirk.

"This is *exactly* what I meant."

This time he was the fast one, closing the distance between them with two long strides. It had been too long since he'd held her. Too long since he'd run his hands across her bare skin. Too long since he'd tasted her.

Now he was going to make up the time lost.

Madi moaned against his lips as they finally

skipped past the sweet and went straight for the hard. Desire thronging through Julian. So powerful he wound his hand in her hair and held Madi fast against his lips. When she lashed her tongue out, deepening it, Julian lost it.

He needed her.

Now.

It was a feeling that was reciprocated.

As he went for the hook of her bra, Madi reached for the button on his jeans. Neither broke their kiss. Both were successful.

Madi spilled out of her bra just as she tugged down on his pants. Julian had to step back then. Madi groaned. Then she looked mad as a kicked hornet's nest.

"What are you—"

He held up a finger to stop her from complaining. With his pants unbuttoned, he scanned the space for anything remotely soft. While he had no problem making love to a pregnant Madi, he couldn't help but feel protective, too. The loft's floor was old wood, rough and not at all ideal for the moves they were about to be taking pleasure in.

Thankfully, he didn't have to look too long. A box not far from their discarded shirts was partially opened. Over one side was the corner of a flannel something. Julian hurried to it, mindful that his pants were a lot tighter than they had been minutes before, and clapped when he saw it was a blanket.

"Good thinking," Madi said at his shoulder. Julian made sure not to look at her yet. Not until the blanket was down. He wouldn't be able to stop himself again.

The material was soft and thick and perfect for the two of them. Once he laid it out and was satisfied it would keep her comfortable, Julian finally turned to face the mother of his child.

"You are beautiful."

Her face was flushed, her blue eyes were heavenly and her smile was a sweetness he was ready to taste again.

Or maybe it wasn't all sweet. The corner of Madi's lips moved up into a smirk that made his jeans even tighter.

"Take those clothes off and tell me that again."

Julian couldn't help the growl that vibrated out of his chest. He did as he was told.

"Yes ma'am."

"WELL, I HAVE to say, it was nice to yell for *good* reasons instead of bad ones."

Julian chucked.

"Let's just hope Clive was still out in the field with the horses," he said. "Otherwise I feel like your brothers are going to have another talk with me. This time not about guns."

He picked up her shirt off the ground and handed it over. They'd both reclaimed their pants but only after taking at least a half-hour sojourn. Neither had been ready to get up and start moving around. Not after the romp they'd just had. Madi was pretty sure she'd seen stars at one point, maybe the universe being created at another. A small part of her had worried that being pregnant would be a deal breaker for the man. Yet somehow it made everything more intimate. Right after they'd finished, Julian had held her against his chest, a hand protectively placed over her stomach. It had moved her mind and heart from lust to something deeper.

Something she didn't want to think about just yet.

While their time together had been mind-blowingly wonderful, Madi knew they had to go back to their current reality.

They had bigger problems to attend to first.

Still, she couldn't help but feel a bit lighter now. A bit more content, too. She slipped her shirt on and gave him a sly smile.

"What would my brothers even talk to you about? Tell you to keep away so I don't get pregnant?" She pointed to her bump. "Sorry, boys, but that ship has sailed."

Julian laughed and went about dressing. Madi took the time to finally look around the loft.

"You know, when we were kids this is where we used to hang out," she said, moving through the closest stacks of boxes and plastic storage tubs. "This was like our unofficial party place. We'd wait until our parents were asleep and then sneak out and meet our friends here. It's been a while since I've been here, though." The cheer in her words started to ebb. "Not since right after Dad died."

Madi scanned the labels, passing over holiday decorations, old school memorabilia and family heirlooms that had been moved from the original Nash family house after it had flooded yet hadn't made it to the new one. Madi knew what was in all of them. Most of all the boxes in the far corner. They didn't have labels on them. They never would.

Despite years of not visiting the space, her feet led her right up to them.

It was amazing what the sight of a few cardboard boxes could do to a person. Madi's skin crawled. Her stomach hardened. An old ache started to rip through her. It allowed a familiar guilt to follow. Especially when she noticed that two of the boxes were partially opened.

Had she been the only one to avoid this place?

What did that say about her?

Had she pretended to have moved on when she was really just a coward?

A warmth came up behind her. Julian placed his hand on her back. A small yet meaningful gesture that gave her the courage to show him something she should have already told him about.

"Though I *thoroughly* enjoyed what we just did, the real reason why I think I wanted to show you the barn was because of these," she started. "And to give you the rest of my story. Can you grab those two boxes? The ones that are opened?"

Julian didn't question the request and soon had two pieces of the Nash family history on the floor in front of them. She placed her hand on the closest one but didn't look inside yet.

"My dad was a good man, but like I said, he couldn't let go of what happened to us when we were kids. The stress… It killed him. It changed us as a family. Even before Dad died. What had happened just changed us. Caleb became focused, analytical. We couldn't get answers but maybe other people could. He started fighting for the underdogs. If we couldn't get closure, then he could help others get it. Desmond became driven, too. But his focus was more on the aftermath. What happens when those who are hurt are forced to keep going. He wanted to help people live life, even after they'd been dealt a bad hand. He went into the business world and used his wealth to create organizations aimed at helping people move on." Madi smiled, as she always did when she felt the pride of what her brothers had managed to do with their lives. "Declan even changed. He was older when it happened, and even though no one has *ever* even remotely suggested it was his fault that we were taken, it hit him pretty hard, too. Caleb was about closure, Desmond was about moving on, but Declan? He became dedicated to stopping anything before it happened. Protecting our hometown, the county. I couldn't tell you what he wanted to do before that day in the park but there was no doubt in anyone's mind after." Madi wavered. She was getting to her part. The one she had never admitted to anyone else. Julian placed a hand over hers.

"And what about you?" he had to ask. It was the only way to get her to finally say it.

"I became angry." She balled her fist and continued, "At first, I didn't even notice it. No one did. But then in elementary school, when I was ten, Andrés Casas ran up behind me at recess and pulled one of my braids. I still don't remember exactly what happened next other than I snapped." Madi sighed in defeat, tears starting to well up in her eyes. "He had to be taken to the hospital and I just broke. I became more impulsive and mean. I had problems trusting people and then connecting. Honestly, I think it drove Dad harder to find the man who attacked us. Why he couldn't let it go or move on. He thought solving the case would fix me."

"PTSD doesn't have one easy fix."

Madi looked into his eyes, surprised.

"No, it doesn't," she said after a moment. "Thankfully, Mom could see I needed help and so she got it for me. For all of us. We went to therapy, participated in a lot of different methods for children who had been through trauma. And eventually, I felt better. I started socializing again, evened out, and then one day would go by and I wouldn't think about what had happened. Then another would go by and then another. I'd be lying if I said there weren't hard moments, but for the most part, I thought I'd moved on."

Madi smiled, knowing it didn't reach her eyes.

"I think—I think a part of me still has a hard time connecting," she said. "It's easier to have walls built up than to try your chances outside, you know?" She ran a hand over her stomach. "But I don't want to be like that anymore. *So...*"

Madi leaned over the top of the closest box and started to rummage through it. She spied what she was looking for near the bottom. Julian was nice enough to bend over and get it for her. When he straightened he gave her an expectant look.

"These boxes hold reminders of our family's tragedies, from Dad's investigation to things that happened during the struggle after." She smiled again. This time she felt more of a warmth in it. She had finally gotten to her point, finally bared a part of herself to Julian that she had never shown anyone else. "But you can only box something up and hide it for so long, and I don't want to keep a big part of my life hidden anymore. Not from you."

Julian's face softened. He looked at the photo album in his hands. It held pictures from the bad years, as Madi thought of them. Yet growing older was a funny thing. Becoming a mother was another interesting twist. Both gave her a perspective she hadn't had before. One that made her appreciate the fact that, while she wished things could have been different sometimes, the life she had now was formed by those bad years.

Without them she wouldn't have met Julian.

She wouldn't be carrying their daughter.

As if on cue with her thoughts, Julian closed the space between them again with a soft kiss. Instead of pulling right away, he lingered.

"You are an extraordinary woman, Madeline Nash."

Madi felt her smile grow. Now it reached her eyes.

"You're not so bad yourself."

Madi decided it was time to take the photo album instead of pretending it didn't exist. They left the loft with Julian holding it fast against his side. A wave of emotions rolled over her at the sight. At everything that just happened between them.

Julian hadn't judged her for her past. For her anger. He'd understood it and accepted it.

What did that mean for them?

What happened next?

"Madi! Madi!"

The sound of yelling took every good and confused thought about her and Julian's future and threw it skyward. She whirled around next to the SUV. Julian was already in front of her, a barrier to keep her safe.

Clive came rushing out of the barn, phone pressed to his ear. He skidded to a stop in front of them, out of breath.

"What's going on?" Julian asked.

Clive held up his finger and took in a few breaths. He must have run in hard from the fields. The man was only a few years older than Madi and in great shape. Whoever was on the phone at his ear was talking loudly but he didn't appear to be affected by it.

"Molly just—just heard that something big happened in Loraine's case," he managed. Clive's wife, Molly, helped run the retreat. She was as plugged into the community as the Nash matriarch. According to Molly, she didn't spread gossip. She spread the truth. "They found something in what was left after the coroner's van was destroyed in the fire."

The hair on the back of Madi's neck started to stand. Clive straightened and looked as severe as Julian did.

"The body Carl and Lee were transporting wasn't Loraine Wilson."

Chapter Sixteen

"Someone switched the bodies before transport," Madi said. Her brother Desmond shook his head.

"There was a deputy with the body while it was stored in the hospital's morgue. Nobody wanted to risk a chain-of-custody issue, especially with you as a suspect and all the possible conflicts of interest. He only left its side when Detective Holloway showed up. Not to mention there are several cameras throughout the hospital that show no one tampering with the body. Definitely not switching it for another." Desmond sighed. "Caleb sneaked off and called me after he finished going through the footage himself."

"Did Detective Holloway have anything to add?" Julian asked. They were back in Desmond's kitchen. Desmond had been quick to confirm Clive's information when they'd come back. Small towns really did have an efficient rumor mill. "Maybe they stopped at a gas station?"

Desmond shook his head again. He'd relinquished his cowboy hat as they started to discuss the newest confusing piece of evidence. Now he ran his hand through his hair in exasperation.

"They never stopped until they were run off the road."

"By the man and the woman," Madi spelled out. Desmond nodded.

"'An eye for an eye' is what Caleb said she told Holloway. Because there aren't already enough stereotypical bad guys in the world without adding clichés."

Madi's eyebrows drew together in thought. Julian wished he had answers for her. For all of them. The other body found in the coroner's van had been confirmed as Carl's. Past that, Julian had nearly forgotten about the van attack, especially after the men had visited the inn. Now they were losing answers and gaining more questions.

"So what you're saying is the woman found at the inn *wasn't* Loraine to start with?" he asked to get them back on track.

Desmond sighed.

"That's the thought," he said. "They found a metal plate in the body with a registration number. It was linked back to a woman named Kathy Smart. Last I heard they were tracking down as much information on her as possible. I think she lives in Manhattan but Caleb didn't know more yet." He lowered his voice a little. "We're not supposed to know any of this, but considering that this case has done nothing but affect our family, he wanted us to know. We can't tell anyone else."

Julian agreed.

"Does Kathy Smart ring any bells for you?" he asked Madi. Maybe she had been a former guest?

The beautiful blonde shook her head. Her hair was already in two braids over her shoulders.

"I know it would be presumptuous of me to think that I know everyone in Overlook but, honestly, I know most," Desmond said. "I've never heard of a Kathy Smart, either."

"So what was she doing at a bed-and-breakfast all the way in Tennessee?" Julian supplied.

Madi readjusted herself in her chair, fingers splayed across her belly.

"I'll raise you one better," she said. "If the body I found is Kathy Smart, then where is Loraine?"

A moment of silence settled in the kitchen. There were so many questions going around that Julian hadn't yet gotten to that one.

"I'm assuming Nathan Wilson is being brought back in for questioning?" he asked. "Don't they usually look at the spouse first when a disappearance or homicide happens?"

Madi nodded.

"Unless there's someone else who jumps out at them first," she said dryly. "Wait, were they able to tell time of death?"

Another question Julian hadn't thought to ask yet.

"The coroner originally guessed two to three hours. I don't think that's changed, either."

"So whoever Kathy was, she was most likely killed in Overlook," Julian postulated.

Desmond nodded.

"With Dad's shotgun no less."

Madi's body tensed. Julian opened his mouth to ask what was wrong when Desmond's phone started to ring in his pocket. He pulled it out and frowned at the caller ID.

"This is work. I took the week off but apparently Jared doesn't understand what that means."

He excused himself and went outside to talk— a habit that all the Nash family seemed to share. They liked being out in the air, day or night.

"What is it?" Julian asked once the back door was closed. Madi's brow was still crinkled. She was staring at the tabletop but Julian could see the gears moving as she thought through what was bothering her.

"Dad's gun." Madi groaned. "Oh crap."

"What about it?"

She hung her head and sighed.

"You know how I said pregnancy brain was real and sometimes it makes my memory into scrambled eggs?"

Julian snorted at that. "I recall."

Madi pushed her chair back and struggled to

stand. She moved closer to him until her round belly touched him.

"After I found the shotgun all I could think about was the last time we argued about it."

"We?"

She lowered her voice.

"Us Nash siblings are pretty close. Like, that's our *thing*. But there are a few fights we've never resolved. One of them was Dad's gun. See, it's kind of a family heirloom, passed down to my father from his, who also got it from *his* father. Originally it was supposed to go to Declan, but after Dad died, he decided he didn't want it for whatever reason. So it was supposed to go to the next eldest Nash kid." She pressed her thumb to her chest. "Which is me, *but* Caleb and Desmond freaked out. Said I was a girl and I couldn't have it—you know, typical sibling rivalry stuff—and that just made me so grumpy! Ma said until we could stop fighting about it she would keep it in her attic. After it was found at my place I told them that's where it was supposed to be and they came and looked around." She covered her mouth. Her eyes widened. She spoke around her hand. "But that's not the last place it was."

Julian felt his eyebrow rise.

"You moved it," he guessed.

Madi nodded, guilt written all over her face.

"I moved it last year and totally spaced about

it." She groaned again. "Oh God, how do I keep looking more and more guilty? If I was me I would arrest me, too!"

Julian grabbed her shoulders and chuckled.

"You just had a lot more than most thrown at you in a very short amount of time. Pregnancy brain or not, I don't think anyone would blame you for forgetting a few things."

"Miller would blame me. He'd do it in a second. It proves I was the *only* person who knew where it was. But also, what if there's evidence there that could answer something?"

Julian sobered. She was right.

"Then let's go check it out and see," he said, rubbing her arms to try to calm her. "There's probably nothing, but at least we can put it out of our minds. Okay?"

Madi took a deep breath.

"Okay."

"Good. Now, where exactly did you hide it?"

Julian watched with equal parts amusement and concern as Madi's face turned a lovely shade of red.

"It's on the ranch but in a very, very petty place. Let's just say I'm not proud."

THEY DROVE TO the opposite side of the ranch, following a dirt road that was well-worn but still gave them a bumpy ride until it dead-ended next to a sign that read Juniper Shoulder.

"This starts a stretch of woods that has two trails you can follow to the mountain or to the creek. We had to mark it before the retreat opened." Madi placed her hand on the top of the sign after they got out of the SUV. "But before the retreat and even before what happened when we were eight, Juniper Shoulder was one of our favorite spots to play." She waved him to follow. Julian met her pace and then slowed to keep it.

"We promised no trails," he reminded her, eyes already roaming their surroundings. The gun the Nash brothers had given him was back in his waistband but he still wasn't enthused about not having a complete sight line around them.

"We're not going that far in. We might have been adventurous when we were kids but we never went too far in."

True to her word, less than five minutes passed and they veered off the trail's path. A hundred or so feet later and Julian was looking at a wooden sign nailed to a tree. There was unintelligible writing across it. Madi translated.

"'No Girls Allowed.'"

Julian cracked a smile.

Madi crossed her arms over her chest.

"We might be a set of triplets but Des and Caleb still teamed up on me sometimes like jerks." He followed her around the tree and a few more feet. Madi stopped and pointed. Julian couldn't help but laugh.

"A tree house. You hid the gun from them in your childhood tree house."

She moved her index finger side to side.

"I hid the gun in the tree house I wasn't allowed in," she corrected. "In my mind, at the time, it was the equivalent of giving them the middle finger for bucking tradition just because I was a girl." She let out a long breath. It deflated her. "They would have told me if they'd found it and moved it."

"Which begs the question, how did the killer know where it was?"

The tree house was impressive. Held up and built around three trees close together, it had obviously been made by someone who knew what they were doing. Julian didn't ask but he assumed that Madi's father had been the one behind it. Even after all these years the stairs that led up to the small structure were still solid. Julian led the way up with Madi close behind.

"After the attack we stopped coming out here. It just wasn't fun anymore," she explained. "The last time we were out here all together was right after Dad passed. There's a trunk inside where we used to keep our toys. I added a combo lock when I put the shotgun there. One with an important but totally unguessable combo." Julian wasn't going to ask but Madi shared the information anyways. "It's Kurt Russell's birthday."

Julian laughed as he pushed open the door, still wildly impressed by the craftsmanship of the house. It wasn't huge but it was big enough that playing inside must have been fun.

Madi started to tell him about how the roof was put on but Julian had stopped in his tracks just inside the door.

"Don't touch anything," he ordered. It was a little too harsh but it did the trick. He felt Madi tense behind him. "Go back down and, Madi, *don't touch anything*. Not even the trees."

Madi didn't question him. A part of Julian felt guilty at his commanding tone but he was doing it for her own good. Once she was back on solid ground, he stepped deeper into the room.

It was the size of a shed, smaller than the Jansens' but still wide and tall enough that Julian and Madi could have walked around without bumping into each other or the ceiling. Like she said, there was a trunk against the opposite wall. A broken combo lock was on the floor next to it.

Between it and him was what made him order Madi back.

Across the floor and sprayed across the wall was dried blood…and other bits.

Julian cursed low and long.

He pulled his phone out and took several pictures before carefully backing out of the small house. He ran a hand across his jaw, then cursed again as he stopped in front of Madi. Her face had gone pale. She clutched at her stomach.

"We're going to have to call Detective Miller, aren't we?" she said, close to a whisper. Dread underlined each word. Julian felt it in his chest, too.

He nodded and showed her the pictures.

"I think it's a safe bet that Kathy Smart was killed in there."

Madi crumpled against him. Julian kept her up with his arms, pulling her into an embrace he knew would do little to help the situation.

"Julian, I'm the only one who knew the gun was here," she cried. Her body stiffened. She raised her head. "I know everything keeps pointing to me but I swear I didn't kill her. I swear it!"

Julian leaned forward and pressed a kiss into her forehead.

"I know you didn't do it," he assured her. "But you weren't the only one who knew where the gun was. Someone else had to have known. And if you didn't tell anyone where you put it, then—"

"Then someone must have followed me."

Julian tried not to let his body tense. He nodded, gaze sweeping the trees around them.

"But why?" she asked into his chest.

More than anything, Julian wished he could give her an answer. He wished he could make it

all better. Assuage her worries and take her to bed
and give her some pleasure in place of the pain
that seemed to keep finding its way to her.

But instead, he was about to invite more worry
and pain.

"We have to call Miller. The longer we don't,
the worse it's going to look."

Madi nodded against him.

"I know," she whispered, her voice so small.
"I'll do it."

Yet she didn't pull away.

And he didn't let her go.

As far as Julian was concerned, for a few minutes they were the only two people in the world.

Chapter Seventeen

Madi flipped through the photo album with every intention of ignoring the lump of guilt growing in her stomach. She should have remembered the tree house.

"So you've always been a braid kind of girl," Julian commented from the driver's seat. To his credit, whether or not he was pretending that everything was okay until Detective Miller arrived, he was paying rapt attention to every photo she flipped through.

The one beneath her fingers now had Declan, Caleb and Madi on horseback. Desmond was a speck in the distance on his own horse. They had no idea that a few weeks later all of their smiles would be strained or lost. Most of the pictures were like that. Which was why they'd found themselves in a box in the loft.

"I definitely get it from my mama," Madi said, mindful to keep her voice light. There was already a long list of things to be depressed about.

"I can count on my hands how many times I've seen her hair down."

Julian smiled.

"Bethany, my little sister, asked me to learn how to do a French braid so I could do her hair when we were teens." Madi gave him a questioning look. He chuckled. "I'm the more coordinated of the two of us. She's book smart like no one's business, but when she has to use her hands for something she's just about the clumsiest person I've ever seen." He held up his index finger and lifted his shirt. He pointed to a small scar on his side. It was thin and faded. Madi had already noticed it, along with several others. She'd never prodded for explanations, just like he'd never asked about the one across her cheek.

"When we were in high school there was this huge party going on at Stacy DeLuca's house," he continued. "I wanted to go because of Stacy's friend Krista, and then Bethany told me it would be social suicide if she didn't go. Problem was, our parents had already said no. But, like in all teen movies—"

"You sneaked out," Madi guessed with a laugh.

"We tried to sneak out." He rolled his eyes. Madi could almost picture teen rebel Julian. "Our bedrooms were on the second floor and the stairs and front door were impossible to get past without waking our parents. So we opted for the bedroom window. There was a big oak tree near it and, honestly, I can still remember how easy it was to jump on it and climb down. But not Bethany. She decides that she's going to freak out halfway down. I mean screeching like you couldn't believe." Julian laughed. "Now, I'm a big guy. Even as a teen I seemed like I was a foot taller than everyone, but Bethany is this little doll-looking human and weirdly fast. It was like trying to get a cat out of a tree." He ran his fingernail along the scar. "And this is what it looks like when a teenage cat decides to not take your hand and falls halfway down the tree but not before scrambling to grab on to something." He shook his head. "She even ripped my shirt."

"I'm assuming she was okay?"

He rolled his eyes again.

"Yeah, yeah. She was fine," he answered. "We were as good as busted, though. Didn't make the party and became prisoners in our home for two months."

Madi laughed.

"I would have liked to see young rebel Julian Mercer."

He chuckled and lowered his shirt. His bandages from their attacker's knife looked out of place against the toned skin of his stomach. It made Madi's mood plummet.

"You know, I don't know much about your life

but I feel like you've been forced into a crash course about mine."

Julian's expression softened.

"You know plenty. You know me. There's always time to learn the rest." He placed his hand over hers. Madi felt a part of her melting at the contact. "Now, show me another picture of Madi before she dyed her hair."

That surprised a laugh out of her.

"Hey, being a triplet can make it hard to feel like an individual. I did what needed to be done." She winked. "And don't act like you aren't a fan of my magical golden hair."

Julian laughed and then was back to focusing on the photo album. They went past more pictures of family before they got into the ones that Madi hadn't seen in a long time.

She said as much as they stopped on a picture that had a group of kids in it.

"This was actually toward the end of my anger issues." She ran her finger across the plastic sleeve over the six kids. They were standing around a long-burned-out fire pit. Madi stood in the middle with her arms crossed. Despite her defensive stance, she was smiling. "It was like a support group for kids who had been through trauma. Once a week for, I think, two months? I can't remember exactly. Caleb and Des didn't go because I think they wanted to see how I would do without them." She hoped she looked apologetic. "I was not the nicest kid in the beginning but I turned it around toward the end." She pointed to the girl at her elbow. "I still talk to Gina occasionally, but that's it."

Madi was about to point out the two kids in the group who had absolutely hated her when a truck appeared on the road behind them. She put the photo album down and tried to steady her nerves. Speaking of people who hated her...

Detective Miller hopped out of his truck with a scowl. He adjusted his belt and turned that scowl toward the trees. His badge shone in the daylight. The butt of his gun from its holster did, too.

"Detective Devereux isn't with him," she said. "He definitely won't be impartial without someone to balance him out."

"Oh, don't you worry," Julian said, opening his door. "I'll balance him out if I have to."

Miller's mood soured the closer they got to him. Madi hadn't seen him since the hospital. He hadn't talked to her then. That had been Devereux. Madi's stomach knotted again. Miller wasn't going to give her any benefit of the doubt.

"This better be good," he greeted. "While y'all have been relaxing out here we've been trying to do work."

Julian played it cool. Cooler than Madi. His body language was relaxed, no aggressive tension. No combative stance. Madi, on the other hand, balled her hands at her sides and clenched her teeth.

"This is something you need to see," Julian explained. "Which is why we immediately called you."

Miller snorted.

"I'm sure only after you called everyone on the ranch."

"You can check our phones," Madi butted in. "You were the only person we called."

That seemed to get a bit more of his attention. Still, he continued to wear the scowl like it was a summer hat. He moved his hand back so it was near his gun and nodded toward the woods.

"Then lead the way."

Julian waited for Madi to strike out first before putting himself between her and Miller. The detective seemed so small compared to him. It made Madi feel better. Yet that momentary relief ended before they ever made it to the tree house, especially since she'd finished recounting the triplet feud about the shotgun.

And that she had hidden it.

And forgotten to tell anyone.

Miller had stopped walking when she was through. He looked like a dog with a bone. His eyes brightened and then immediately narrowed.

"Are you kidding me?" he said, dangerously

near a shout. "You just happened to forget key information about *the murder weapon*?" He shook his head. "Do you Nashes think you're above the law? That it can't touch you because you've been through some bad stuff in your lives?"

Madi's nerves hardened. Then they were glowing hot.

"This has *nothing* to do with what happened when we were kids," she yelled, not bothering in the least to keep calm. "I'm sorry that after finding a body and immediately being fingered as the murderer, a detail slipped my mind." She pointed to her stomach. "You try creating a kid, running a business, having to take crap from a lawman who clearly wants you to fry and then trying to keep everything in line. Two weeks ago I spent an hour trying to find my damn keys *that were in my hand*!"

"Don't compare this to losing your keys!"

"And don't forget I didn't have to tell you I'd remembered this at all," she shot back. "But here we are, shouting so close to the front of a crime scene you still haven't seen because you're too busy yelling at me!"

That shut him up. Miller's nostrils flared. He looked between Madi and Julian with what she guessed was barely contained rage. Julian was no longer carrying himself with a cool relaxation, either. He was mad, too. The three of them certainly were quite the trio. They didn't speak until the tree house was in front of them.

"Don't you two move," Miller finally bit out.

"Wouldn't dream of it."

Madi wanted to say more but Julian took her hand. It defused her next outburst before it could come out. They watched in silence as Miller disappeared inside the tree house.

"You didn't do it, Madi," Julian said. "I'm not going to let anyone say otherwise."

There was a severity to his words. A strength that was as intimidating as it was comforting.

Madi tried to hang on to that feeling as Miller finally came back out.

For the first time since she'd known the man, Madi couldn't read his expression. He descended the stairs without saying a word. Julian dropped her hand.

"Madi wouldn't have needed to break that combo lock that was on the trunk," he pointed out. "Whoever did that is the person you're looking for. She also didn't go inside today. Only I did."

Miller didn't respond.

At least not in words.

When he was right in front of them his eyes went over their shoulders and widened. Julian was quick to turn, body tensing and ready to deal with whatever came their way, but Madi was slower.

She watched in shock as Detective Miller pulled

his gun out and smacked it against Julian's head. It was the perfect blow. Just as the man in the woods had done to her when she was eight.

Julian hit the ground hard.

He didn't move.

A scream of anger escaped Madi before she realized that the gun was now pointed at her.

"You're going to listen to me right now or all *three* of you die."

EVERYTHING WAS WET.

His hair. His skin. His clothes. The ground.

It was raining.

Julian's face was pressing into dirt that had become mud. It oozed across his cheek and stung his eye. Not that the mild annoyance was more concerning than the throb of pain at the back of his head. He'd been knocked out.

"Madi!" Julian tried to bring his hands up to help him push off the ground but came up short. They were bound.

They were *handcuffed*.

Julian let out a guttural sound. It was primal. It was protective.

"Madi," he yelled again.

He rolled onto his back and sat up. It wasn't a downpour but the drops were thick and heavy. They pelted the ground with force. Julian could no more see tracks across the ground as he could see the two people who might have made them.

Miller.

Julian rocked back enough to get momentum, then jumped up to his feet. It was a trick he'd made a point to learn since his buddies from his unit had said Lumberjack was too big to be that fluid. Now the trick got him to his feet and moving. He ran full tilt up the tree house stairs, heart in his throat, before kicking the door down. It didn't take much but Julian felt like he could tear down steel if it meant getting to Madi.

The dried blood was still splattered across the room but the combo lock was gone. So were Madi and Miller.

He was both relieved and pissed as hell.

If Miller had taken Madi then it meant she could be still alive.

Julian turned on his heel, words vile and anger filled spilling out of his mouth like the rain off his shirt. He ran back to the trail and out through the woods.

His SUV was gone. So was Miller's truck.

Julian kept on running.

Chapter Eighteen

The rain didn't let up. It made Julian's several-mile trek even more of a pain. At one point he had to stop, lie on his back, move his wrists under the back of his legs, around his feet, and stand so that his cuffed hands were in front of him. It was still constricting but made for much easier movement. He needed to be ready for anything.

Even though he hadn't been earlier.

Focus, he thought bitterly. *You have to find them.*

The pain in Julian's head and the burn in his legs and lungs were at an all-time high by the time the Wild Iris Retreat's cabins came into view. At least, he assumed that was what the cluster of small buildings were. He hadn't been given a proper tour yet and the rain was making it difficult to see or read any signage. He'd barely seen the lights on in one of the cabins until he was almost up to the front porch.

He ran up the stairs three at a time. A plaque

next to the door declared the building was Cabin 3. It wasn't until Ray flung open the door after he pounded against it that Julian realized the guest had been thrown right back into the thick of things. Madi might have worried what that would mean for the future of Hidden Hills but Julian was worried only for her and their child. If that meant throwing Ray into the middle of a gunfight as his backup, Julian would do it in a heartbeat.

"My God, what's going on?" Ray asked, eyes zipping to the cuffs and then back up.

"Madi was taken by Detective Miller," Julian said, jumping in. "He knocked me out and restrained me. I woke up and they were gone. So were my phone, gun and vehicle."

Ray's eyes widened in acute surprise. He motioned Julian inside, shaking his head in disbelief.

"The detective heading up the case about Loraine? Why would he do that?"

Julian growled.

"A question I plan to ask him myself the next time I see him. Until then I need to call the department."

Ray grimaced. He hesitated and then held up his phone and shook it.

"I don't know how long you were out, but you must have missed the big show." He pointed to the window. "The storm got really rough there for a second. I'm guessing it damaged the cell tower that serves this area. No calls are coming in or going out. I'm surprised we even have power after all of that."

Julian cocked his head to the side. That was a small hitch in his plan. He wiped at the water falling from his hair into his eyes. The handcuffs clinked together at the movement.

"I need you to drive me to the department. I need to talk to the sheriff immediately. He has to know that Miller has gone rogue."

Ray grimaced again.

"My car is still at Hidden Hills."

Julian gave the man a flat stare.

"What?"

Ray shrugged, apologetic.

"Since the investigation at the inn, I was shuttled here. I haven't really missed having a car since I just stay on the ranch. I was told I could wait to get it on my way out of town if I wanted."

Well, that was more than a hitch in his plan than Julian wanted.

Ray held up his hand.

"But what I can do is get us into the retreat's main office. I don't think Nina or the other manager is there right now. It should have a landline, though!"

A loud clap of thunder backed up his offer. It sent a powerful feeling of foreboding into his bones. He hoped wherever Madi was, she was inside. She had joked about them having bad luck and now Julian was tempted to agree. Clear skies sure would have helped tip the scale somewhat back into their favor. Or at least make finding her easier.

Case in point, Julian was having a hard time just keeping the rain out of his eyes while inside. Running through the rain might have been thematic but it wasn't at all practical.

Ray seemed to agree. He eyed the growing puddle beneath Julian and pointed to the opposite side of the cabin.

"Let me grab us some towels first. They won't fix the downpour out there but maybe they'll help some."

Julian would have turned him down but his run was catching up to him. He was hurting, but even harder to ignore was how thirsty he was.

"I need some water."

The cabin only had three rooms. The living space, the bedroom and the attached bathroom. All small but functional. A tiny kitchenette was tucked in the corner of the living area with a little refrigerator and a sink. Julian was at the sink, head bent under the faucet, in seconds. Once the water hit his lips, he could have sung.

He had never tasted anything sweeter.

Julian drank like a man who had just crawled out of the desert and angled his head to get a better fix on the water. It put the miniature dining table directly in his sight line. A quaint round table with two wooden chairs tucked beneath with a vase and flowers on its top.

And next to it, a leather-bound book.

Julian cut the water off and stood.

Not a book. A photo album. One he'd seen before.

He went to the table and assured himself he was mistaken. Surely it wasn't the one he was thinking of and instead was a guest book, or maybe Ray had bought it as a souvenir.

Julian's adrenaline surged. He flipped the book open.

Three children standing arm in arm smiled up at him. The little girl in the middle had one braid thrown over each shoulder. There was no scar on her cheek yet.

"I'm sorry I don't have anything more helpful than towels," Ray said from the other room. "But I feel like we can better help her if we're not drenched to the bone."

Julian closed the album and moved back to the sink. He gave Ray a curt nod as the other man appeared with two towels. One look at Julian and his eyebrows drew in together.

"Are you okay? The detective didn't shoot or cut you, did he?"

Julian shook his head, careful to keep his expression as neutral as possible. Even if he was two seconds away from grabbing the man and trying to shake information out of him.

Why did Ray have the photo album they'd gotten from the loft? The one that had been in Julian's SUV when they'd gone into the woods?

"Just a solid hit to the head. Nothing I can't power through."

Ray's eyebrow arched. A ripple of hesitation moved across his expression. Julian's almost-spent leg muscles tensed further. The cabin's charming facade crumbled. Now it was a possible staging area for a fight. One in which Julian already had a disadvantage with his hands restrained. Fighting in nothing but a towel hadn't been ideal; fighting with both hands bound was a stone's throw away from very, very bad luck.

"Well, we better get going, then," Ray said after a moment. "Let me just grab my key to the lobby."

Julian was curious about the game Ray was obviously playing. What was his plan? Play nice until they got to the phone? Or was the man waiting for an opening to take on Julian?

"I'm ready when you are," Julian said, changing his stance to provide more stability. Ray bent over a pair of jeans that was tossed over the couch's arm.

"You said no one knows?" Ray asked, rooting around the pockets for his keys. Julian noted that they were dark on the bottom of the legs. Wet. "I mean, about you and Madi going out to the trail in the first place?"

Julian clenched his jaw. If he hadn't seen the photo album his internal alarm bells would have been ringing at that. He hadn't said anything about a trail.

And Ray was taking awfully long looking for his keys.

"As far as I know."

Julian tightened his grip on the towel, wishing he had full use of his hands. It would have to do.

Up until now Julian had never really tried to get a read on Ray. There hadn't been a need. He was pleasant enough, quiet. Average, according to Madi's observation. Julian had agreed. But now he realized that Ray could have crafted this persona by design, and Julian wasn't wearing rose-colored glasses anymore. Now Julian saw a man who could get lost in a crowd with ease. A man who showed interest and skill in the outdoors.

A man who was still wearing his riding gloves and favoring his left hand.

Julian went through everything he knew about the case so far. His thoughts flew past Ray and to the death of the coroner. Detective Holloway's description of the man and woman who had taken him was generic. He'd claimed the man had black hair. Ray didn't, but Julian wasn't ruling him out on hair color alone. Not when Holloway had said he'd shot the man in the hand.

"It might be easier to find the keys if you took off the gloves."

It was clear Ray was now stalling. Still, he kept fishing for them, finally making it to the back pockets. Julian glanced around the other surfaces in the room. He wasn't surprised when he spotted the keys next to the door. Ray was definitely stalling. Julian leaned into it.

"You know, I wanted to apologize for everything you've been through while here in town," he started. "A murder wasn't exactly what Madi had in mind for her guests' experience."

"It wasn't her fault," Ray brushed off. He moved to the last pocket.

"I'm surprised I didn't run into you before today, though. I had to spend a long time at the department giving Madi's alibi. If you don't mind me asking, what was yours?"

Ray stopped. He slid his hand out of the pocket and stood to his full height. Another surge of adrenaline shot through Julian's system. His heart was hammering away, as if competing with the storm outside. For a moment the two of them just stared.

Then the sound of a cell phone ringing filled the room.

Julian wondered what else the man had lied

about just as Ray's pleasant persona faded into a smirk.

"We both know that neither one of us had an alibi."

Ray reached around for something in the back of his waistband. Julian wasn't going to wait to see what that was. He ran the distance between them and lowered his shoulder before impact.

He'd been here before. The last two fights he'd encountered were a surprise. This one had the bonus disadvantage of his hands being bound. Julian didn't need to survive this fight. He needed to stop it before it started.

Something clattered to the ground as Julian slammed Ray against the front door. It was a harder hit than Julian had bargained for. Even though the door hadn't been properly shut when they'd first come in, it crashed open with such force that something cracked. The momentum carried them across the small porch and right to the top of the stairs.

Ray groaned as his back took the brunt of their fall. Julian rolled off the man but didn't stand. Julian moved into a crouch and grabbed the collar of Ray's shirt. He fisted the cloth and pulled the man up enough that if he had to, he could slam his head back onto the porch.

"Where is she?" Julian yelled. "Where's Madi?"

Ray coughed, squeezing his eyes shut and trying to catch his breath. Julian wasn't about to show the man sympathy. He shook him.

"Where is Madi?"

"I—I—" Ray tried. He opened his eyes. They were angry. "I'm big—big picture. I've never been good at the details."

Julian felt the tension beneath his knuckles just before Ray struck. He might have been a smaller man than Julian but the movement was surprisingly effective. His head hit Julian's nose so hard that he knew it was busted before he ever saw the blood or felt the pain.

"Son of a—"

Julian recoiled but refused to let the head butt send him to the ground. He rocked on his heels, tensed his leg muscles and managed to spring up instead. It gave Ray the opening to roll over and get to his feet.

"You messed this up," he growled. "You—"

Julian intertwined his fingers and struck out, envisioning his joined hands as a sledgehammer. Ray yelled out. He danced backward and right off of the porch. Once again he hit the ground, this time on his side. He devolved into another fit of coughing. Julian jumped the stairs and landed next to him, adrenaline coursing through him with purpose. His head, nose and shoulder throbbed in pain. The rain drenched their clothes.

Though it was Julian's heart that was the loudest.

"Where is she?" he yelled. "I won't ask again."

Ray struggled to get up. Julian wasn't going to let him. Not without answers.

"Let him go!"

Julian never even heard her walk up. He turned around. A woman with dark blond hair had a gun pointed at him. Just far enough away that he'd be a goner if he lunged for it.

Had she been in the cabin the entire time?

"Move away from him," she added. "Or you're dead."

"How many of you are there?" Julian asked in anger. He did as she said but stepped behind Ray so his back wasn't to the man. "Every time I turn around there's someone else with a gun and a snappy line."

The woman smirked.

"I'm sorry we're inconvenient, but at least now you know how it feels."

She motioned to the cabin.

"Now, go inside. Slowly," she ordered, voice clear through the downpour. "Or a snappy line will be the last thing you hear."

Bad luck really did seem to be the theme of the day. Julian weighed his options again. Fight and flight both resulted in the high possibility of being shot...which he was hoping to avoid.

He couldn't help Madi if he was hurt. Or worse.

Julian raised his hands slowly and nodded. The

woman moved aside, careful to keep the gun's aim true. Ray continued to cough and sputter. A few profanities found their way out into the rain before Julian could clear the cabin's front door.

He clocked all of the exits he could see and guessed at the ones he couldn't. He noted the lamp, a horse statue on the entryway table and the cabinet drawer where he would guess the cutlery was stashed. The couch was between it and him. He could use it for cover if needed.

"Don't get any ideas," the woman called from behind.

Too bad that was exactly what he was doing.

"Who are you?" he asked, eyes falling back to the small horse statue. It looked like it was made of metal and had a substantial amount of heft to it. It was no cell phone or pair of handcuffs, but he'd be able to use it if needed. "Where's Madi?"

The woman's laugh was biting. Julian stopped next to the entryway table and turned. Standing in the doorway with the light against her face and the rain at her back, she was a confusing sight.

Mostly because she was Loraine. Even beneath her blond wig, Julian recognized the face from the picture he'd been shown at the sheriff's department.

"I don't know, but I suspect I will soon enough," she said, smiling through dark red lips.

Ray walked up behind her, slightly hunched over. He held his chest, scowling.

"Careful," he warned.

Loraine snorted.

"He saw the photo album. He knows who I am. I don't think he's going to be quiet about either. Are you, Mr. Mercer?"

Julian kept his mouth shut.

He wasn't confident he could dodge any bullet at this range. Maybe he could take one in the shoulder before he got the gun away from her.

Loraine cocked her head to the side.

"What? Not going to talk now?" She shrugged. "It doesn't matter. The *real* question I want to ask is what's going to make all the difference."

She took a small step forward. It brought her within striking distance. Julian's muscles started to coil, readying. Loraine, however, knew just what to ask to make them freeze.

"How much do you *really* love Madi?"

Chapter Nineteen

Madi heard the rain start but she never saw a drop of it. Instead she'd been held in what she could only assume was an abandoned building in the woods. She'd been tossed into the van outside the Juniper trail and blindfolded. Just as her brothers had been all those years ago. This time she was conscious for the abduction and told not to make a sound. She hadn't. Instead she'd done her best to pay attention.

The ride hadn't lasted more than ten minutes, which meant they were still in Overlook.

Good news, all things considered.

It meant Julian and her brothers stood a chance at finding her.

A vise squeezed in her chest at the image of Julian on the ground. He had been so still.

"Stop moving," Miller snapped, tearing her thoughts away from the man she'd been forced to leave behind. "You're driving me crazy."

Madi rolled her eyes. If she could have reached

her hair, she would have already braided it several times over. The only thing keeping her from devolving into a puddle of fear and memories of being eight and terrified was her daughter. Madi couldn't protect her or herself if her head wasn't clear. She had to keep as much control as she could. Even if, in the back of her mind, she was doing nothing but reassuring herself that she wasn't that scared child anymore. She was a mom. She was strong.

She had to be strong.

A task made more difficult by the man next to her. For the last half hour the detective had been in fine form. She'd never heard a grown man growl as much as he did. It was like being held captive with a grumpy bulldog.

Which wasn't a shock, given his temperament and general dislike of her, but what *was* a shock was Miller being a victim alongside her. She hadn't seen that coming. After he'd knocked Julian out, it had taken her longer than it should have to notice the men coming out of the tree house, guns drawn. She'd been so angry at the detective for attacking the father of her child.

"They said they'd kill us all if I didn't take care of him," Miller had said right after Julian hit the ground. "I'm a fast shot but I can't get them both before they shoot back."

Miller had been ordered to drop his gun and

handcuff Julian before they'd been taken. They moved so fast that Madi hadn't had time to process until they were driving away. After the ride, she and Miller had been dumped in a windowless room, covered in dust, mold and dirt. The only piece of furniture was a weathered wooden bench set up in the middle. One that had become the bane of her existence.

They'd already tried to lift the bulky thing but it was too long and way too heavy. It didn't help matters that their wrists were zip-tied around the middle plank of the seat, palms up. It was an awkward position that neither could get any good leverage with, no matter how much begrudging teamwork they'd tried.

"I'm uncomfortable," Madi countered. "You try being tied to a bench with no backrest and a belly that makes sitting normally uncomfortable and try not to fidget."

Miller let out a loud, gruff sigh.

"There you go with that pregnant stuff again," he said. "We get it. You have a baby in you which makes your problems ten times worse than everyone else's."

Madi sucked in the bad words that immediately sprang to the tip of her tongue. When he wasn't mean, he was sarcastic. Neither was a good look on the man. A point Madi would have loved to make. Yet the truth was that fighting with Miller wasn't going to get her out of the situation. It could only stand to make it worse.

"*They* don't care that I'm pregnant," she said instead. A shiver ran down her back. Her anger at the detective deflated. "Why did they even take us? Both of us, I mean. It doesn't make sense." It was a concern they'd already passed around after realizing that breaking out of their restraints wasn't going to happen. Still, Madi thought it warranted saying again. "You're the law. Taking you only makes everything harder on them, just like when Detective Holloway was missing. Who would voluntarily take that kind of heat?"

Miller sucked on his teeth for a moment. His eyes stayed on the door.

"If these are the men who attacked you and Julian at Hidden Hills—"

"Which they are," she interjected. For the second time since they'd been in the room. "It's hard to forget the faces of the men who threaten to torture you and shoot at you."

"Then I'm assuming their jobs have changed."

"Their jobs?" Madi repeated.

Miller, ever a man to play it close to the vest, seemed to flounder between divulging the information he had and keeping quiet. Madi was ready to give him an aggressive piece of her mind if he didn't spill. Thankfully, he must have decided it was time for everyone to be on the same page.

"Julian said there was a scorpion tattoo on the man who stabbed him," he started with notable reluctance. "There's a gang in Kilwin that has cropped up in recent years that have done a good deal of outsourcing certain jobs so they don't get them linked back to the gang. The group of men they outsource to are rumored to have scorpion tattoos hidden on their bodies. The mayor has been in talks with the chief about making a task force that will be dedicated to tracking them down and putting them behind bars for good, but after the latest budget cuts, it's been tabled until further notice." He took a moment to swear. "I think the men who came at you at Hidden Hills are a part of that group. I think they were hired to get the truth out of you about Loraine's murder."

"But Loraine isn't dead."

"Exactly. Which may be why their tactics have changed."

"They think I know where the real Loraine is," she realized.

Miller nodded.

"That would be my guess."

Madi took a second to chew on that. Her stomach was starting to knot up again. So far she had surprised herself with how calm she was being. The situation was way worse than when she was in the woods, hiding from danger. Now she was in the belly of the beast, waiting for the unknown. A violent unknown, if the other day was any indication.

For the umpteenth time since they'd been tied to the bench, Madi tried to touch her stomach. It was a feeble attempt to protect her child. The plastic of the zip ties bit into her wrists, making her raw skin burn even more. A feeling of defeat spread through her like wildfire. Its flames were fueled by the weight of the lie she'd been holding up. The same one that had tied Julian into the dangerous web she'd found herself in. Even though he had been the one to tell it first, Madi couldn't help but wonder what would have happened had she not gone along with it. If she had told the truth at the department in the first place, would he be okay now? And furthermore, would her child be in this much danger?

Madi did her best approximation of squaring her shoulders. She decided it was time to control what she could.

"I lied about my alibi," she finally said. "Julian showed up when I was being taken into custody for the first time, not before. I was alone in my suite when I found that woman in my bed. Julian only said what he did to protect me when everything started pointing my way." It was her turn to sigh. "But Miller, I didn't kill that woman and I don't know anything about what's happening. That's the honest-to-God truth."

It felt like a weight had been lifted from Madi's chest. It was one less thing to worry about. One less puzzle piece to hold.

Madi waited for the hammer to drop from the detective. For him to gloat about having grounds for arrest. That justice would finally find its way to the Nash family and he'd be the one to do it.

"I believe you."

Madi felt her eyes widen. They shared a look before his eyes dropped to her stomach. Then he was focused back on the door across from them.

"Really?"

"You're legitimately scared for your baby. There's no way in Hades you'd willingly put yourself in the middle of all of this." He shrugged. "Everyone lies at one point or another but there are some things you just can't hide. You wanting to keep that little one safe is ingrained like a reflex. But don't get me wrong, I still think you're more than capable of killing. I just figure you'd at least wait until the kid was born before you did it."

Madi snorted.

"Thanks. I think."

"Don't thank me." He tugged on his own restraints. His skin was past raw. Blood was drying around the plastic. He'd put up much more of a fight than she had. "If they are trying to get information out of us, *not* having that information isn't going to make our lives easier. It just means they're going to try even harder to break us."

Those knots in Madi's stomach multiplied. He was right. She'd told the man with the knife at Hidden Hills that she didn't know anything. That hadn't deterred him. Neither had her pregnancy.

"Julian and my brothers will find us," she rallied.

It was more for her than it was for him.

"I have no doubt that they'll try," he said. "So the new name of the game until someone comes to get us is stalling. If we can't get out then we'll have to buy time for someone to get in. Got it?"

Madi nodded.

"Stalling it is."

They lapsed into silence. It was surreal in a way. There she was, hitched to a bench, next to the only man her father had ever suspected in the triplets' abduction. The same man who had made clear, publicly, that he hated the Nash family and the love that the community had for them. Madi had seen that hate reflected in her father's eyes when talking about Miller. It made a lasting impression on Madi.

She hated the man next to her because of it.

Yet maybe *hate* was too strong a word. He'd been cleared of having any involvement in the abduction and had made a nice career in law enforcement in Kilwin. Most of all, he'd come up with a plan that had spared Julian's life.

Maybe Christian Miller wasn't as bad as her father had believed.

Or maybe Madi's pregnancy hormones were playing tricks on her and Miller was in on the whole thing.

Madi took a deep breath.

Speculating had gotten them nowhere.

The silence stretched for several more minutes before a new sound sliced it clean through.

"Footsteps," Madi whispered. "Someone's coming."

"Remember, stall."

A dead bolt could be heard retracting as the door was unlocked. Madi didn't know which hired baddie she hoped to see once the door was pushed open. The man who had seemed delighted to torture her or the man who hadn't been stingy with ammo when it came to shooting at her.

However, neither man came inside.

"You have *got* to be kidding me," Madi breathed out.

Miller wasn't far behind in his reaction. He swore like the devil.

Nathan Wilson didn't seem at all offended. He smiled delightedly.

"Oh, believe me, the feeling is mutual," he greeted. "I'd much rather pack my bags and get out of this hick town, but you know, I'd like my wife to be with me for that. And now look at where we are."

He made a grand gesture at the room around them. He looked as out of place as Madi felt, wearing a linen suit and brown dress shoes. He just didn't fit in Overlook, a fact that was even more apparent as he gave them a slow once-over. Nathan looked like he was on the way to see the horse races or attend a fund-raiser at the yacht club. Not popping in on two restrained people in some dilapidated and dusty room.

He dropped his hands to his sides and stopped a few feet from them. His gaze went to their wrists before meeting Miller's eyes.

"I'm really sorry you got caught up in this, Detective. Truly. I tried to help you, but this one here, well, she had her own help. Help I didn't bargain for."

"Help me?" Miller asked, back as straight as he could manage given the ties at his wrists. "How were you helping me?"

Nathan fingered a button on his blazer. It was a casual gesture that made the confusing situation even more bizarre.

"I was making sure she didn't get away with it. The murder." He shared a quick look with Madi. She made sure not to avert her gaze. She might not have understood everything going on but she wasn't going to give him the satisfaction of enjoying her fear. "I've done my research on the Nash family," he continued. "I know all about the unsolved case of the Nash children taken at a park. Held for days, only managing to escape by helping one another. A touching yet scary case for a small town, I'm sure. Especially since there have been no leads or suspects. At least, not since you were accused of being connected to the whole thing. Sure, you were absolved of it but that doesn't change what happened. A good cop and citizen had his name dragged through the mud because the accuser came from a family that everyone loved. That's what *you* said in countless interviews and public statements. Behind closed doors, too, as far as I can tell." Nathan shook his head. "I wasn't going to let Loraine's killer go just because her last name is Nash. Even if it meant conducting my own investigation."

"I don't think you can call what you've been doing an investigation," Miller said. "We don't kidnap and threaten people. We don't attack them. What you're doing isn't taking justice into your own hands. You're abusing it because you're frustrated."

Nathan laughed.

"Frustrated? You think I'm frustrated?" He shook his head. "All I am is a husband trying to find his wife since it's clear no one else is doing anything about it. As far as I can tell it's the law enforcement who are the last to know anything around here. Why would I sit around twiddling my thumbs when I could simply reach into my substantially deep pockets and get you the real culprit? The real murderer."

Madi felt her cheeks heat up in anger.

"But I didn't kill anyone," she replied, trying to keep her voice even. A muscle in Nathan's jaw twitched. Madi wasn't the only one trying to keep control of their anger. "You do know that, right? That it wasn't Loraine's body that was found?"

"She's still missing," he shot back. "And there's nothing you can say that can convince me you're not involved."

"So you've been following me?" Madi had to ask, stalling but still trying to find answers. For instance, how in the world his men had managed to ambush them at the tree house. All without being seen. "If you have, then you have to realize I've done nothing that warrants your belief that I'm involved with what's happening."

Nathan actually scoffed.

"I would have been had you not run away to the only place in this godforsaken town that could keep you hidden and safe," he said, annoyance obvious. "Which is why I ordered my men to keep an eye on the one man other than myself who would do anything and everything to see you taken from that safe place." Nathan shared a look with Miller. He actually smiled before turning back to Madi. "When it was clear he was going down Winding Road with purpose, I told them it was time to try to take you two in. My men, they've done their homework about the ranch. The layout. They knew when Detective Miller turned off the main road and turned again. There were only a handful of places he could go, all away from any of the houses. The perfect spot to ambush you all. So they waited long enough so as to not raise suspicion before they had to and then simply drove up and parked their vehicle next to yours like guests ready to do some hiking. I'm not surprised Mr. Mercer didn't hear them following. Then again, I hire the best of the best." He grinned and motioned between Madi and Miller. "I'm told they were ready to take you then, but when your little fight broke out? Well, they used it to help even the odds in their favor. You were all so busy being angry you never even suspected two men were moving around you and into position inside the tree house." He laughed. It was unkind.

"And now you're here to interrogate us," Miller spelled out. It was clear he wasn't happy at having been followed. "To force a confession under duress."

Nathan took a step forward. There was a harsh

glint in his eye that promised he was a man of his word.

"Don't worry, Detective. Remember, I'm on your side," he said. "The only thing you're guilty of is not getting a confession. So I'll get one for you."

The way his smile twisted, coupled with his certainty, left nothing but dread in Madi's stomach. How could she confess to something she didn't do? And even if she did confess, what would happen next?

She wasn't the only one who was wondering the same thing.

"Then what happens next?" Miller asked. "Let's say she tells you what you want to hear—what then? Do you let me take her to the station?"

That wasn't at all what Nathan had planned. Madi saw that as clear as day before he ever shook his head.

"I'm sorry but no, Detective." Nathan got so close Madi could smell his cologne. "We both know we're past that. No, what's going to happen is this." He pointed to Madi. "You're going to tell me what's going on and where my wife is. Then I'm going to go get her." He bent down so his eyes were even with Madi's. "And when Loraine is finally by my side, I'm going to be as surprised as everyone else in this town that Madeline Nash met her end in the same woods that scarred her when she was a child." Madi kept perfectly still as Nathan reached out and traced the scar on her cheek. "And at the hands of the same man her father suspected all those years ago."

He dropped his hand.

"If you're going to kill us anyway, why would we give you anything?" Miller asked. His voice was hard.

Nathan straightened his back, standing to his full height. He smoothed his blazer down and picked invisible lint off the sleeve. It was a more menacing sight than if he'd brandished a weapon and waved it in Madi's face. When he was done, he was smiling for all he was worth.

It terrified her.

"There is nothing either one of you could do to stop the outcome," he said. "Wouldn't you feel better finally doing the right thing before that happens?"

The name of the game was stalling. Madi knew that. Yet all words died on her tongue. She wanted to cradle her stomach; she wanted to tear through Nathan for being so callous. For being so wrong.

Miller didn't respond, either.

Nathan eventually shrugged.

"We'll do this the hard way, then."

For all his pomp and circumstance, Nathan simply left the room. The door shut behind him with a weight Madi felt in her bones. Only after the sound of the dead bolt locking did Miller speak.

"We're most likely in the old storage building at the park. The one that's been closed for years. If they stage it just right it'll look like I brought you here to kill you."

"Julian and my brothers will think I tried to stop you out of self-defense," she offered.

"And that me snapping is what made you do it. All of this starting with me knocking Julian out." Miller sighed. "He's put us all right where he wants us."

Madi's vision started to blur. The tears were fast, but they weren't sad.

No. They were angry.

She wasn't going to let that happen.

Chapter Twenty

He was wet, bloodied, handcuffed and mad as
hell. Quite the sight, Julian was sure, as he ran into
the Nash family's main house. Madi had once said
it was the heart of the ranch. He didn't see how
that was true since she wasn't there, but thankfully, one of her brothers was.

Desmond jumped up from the dining room
table, which had papers stretched out across its
surface, and took in Julian with blue eyes that
only reminded Julian of what he'd lost.

"Julian! What's going on?"

His body protested the walk from the doorway
to the table. After Loraine had posed her question,
Ray had taken the gun from her. Julian didn't know
if he meant to use it or just hold it for the woman
so she could ramp up into a speech. Regardless,
he hadn't stayed around to find out. Julian had
charged them as soon as the gun's barrel was down
and, once again, had thrown Ray's footing off. He'd

used the opening to run as fast as he could into the rain, his mind made up.

He needed backup.

Ray and Loraine hadn't followed. Julian had made the run from the retreat to the main house with determined power in every movement of his muscles, yet the last few steps exhausted him even more.

"Tell your brothers to get here. *Now.*" Julian dropped the soaked pillowcase and plastic bag on the ground. He crouched down and retrieved Madi's photo album. It wasn't wet, a small victory in what now felt like a long war.

Desmond eyed it with confusion but already had his phone out. There was no hesitation in him dialing. Ray had lied about no calls going out. Not that Julian was surprised.

He'd lied about a lot.

"Where's Madi?" Desmond asked. Judging by his expression, Julian knew the man realized it was nothing good. Still, they were working against time. Brevity was the key to getting her back.

"Detective Miller took her," he rushed. "And Loraine and Ray are hell-bent on getting her, too."

Desmond's eyes widened. Anger, worry and pain raced across his face.

Julian knew all three well by now.

TOO MUCH TIME had passed. From the moment he was knocked out until the moment after he'd caught up the Nash brothers and Caleb's partner, Detective Santiago, Julian was able to track the time they had lost. The period between the last time he saw the beautiful woman and the present.

Almost two hours, give or take.

Those were too many minutes. Too many seconds.

Julian, now free of his cuffs and wearing a change of clothes, felt each one of them like the stab of a knife.

They only continued to go by as the detectives and sheriff got on their phones and made several calls. It wasn't until Declan came back in, sheriff's badge pinned prominently to his belt, that the rest filed back into the dining room. There was tense authority behind the man's words as he addressed them all.

"There's an all-points bulletin out on Miller. The same for Loraine and Ray since Ray's cabin didn't have any clues as to where they might be. Officers, deputies, even reserve deputies are all out in force looking for everyone. If they're anywhere in the county, we can find them. Just in case, other departments and stations have been notified."

"And what about Miller? What did the chief say about his detective kidnapping a pregnant woman?" Desmond asked, hot under the collar. "Isn't that a conflict of interest to still have them involved?"

Declan took his cowboy hat off and rubbed the back of his neck.

"This entire thing is a conflict of interest for everyone involved. We're a small county, it happens," he said. "But we need the numbers and, truth be told, I trust the chief. I've never trusted Miller." He cursed. "I should have fought more to have him taken off the case. If he's working with Loraine and Ray, then that means he was involved with the people who shot Holloway."

"Not to mention his potential involvement in our kidnapping when we were kids," Caleb pointed out.

Declan nodded grimly.

"There is that."

Julian didn't feel the same certainty.

"Miller could have killed me," Julian said. "In fact, that would have been the smarter play. I'd seen him. Why not kill me? He had to have known I'd come to you all."

"Maybe he didn't want the mess or the hassle?" Detective Santiago offered. "It's one thing to be a kidnapper—it's another to be a cold-blooded murderer." The Nash brothers turned to her at that. "Sorry," she muttered. "But you know what I mean."

Julian rubbed at the raw skin around his wrists where the handcuffs had been.

"But what about the cars?" he added. "When I came to, both his truck and my SUV were gone. Who drove them? Miller and Madi? I can't imagine he would allow Madi behind the wheel of a car. She would try to escape."

"Loraine and Ray," Caleb said.

That didn't feel right. It hadn't since Julian had first thought about it.

"When I asked Loraine where Madi was she said she didn't know. Yet. Ray also seemed genuinely surprised to see me. Even more so when I said Miller had taken Madi. There's a lot of things you can fake, but true surprise is hard to hide."

"What are you saying?" Caleb asked. "That Loraine and Ray weren't behind Madi being taken by Miller? Or that Miller didn't take her?"

Julian stood. He'd already downed several bottles of water. Still, he knew the next day he'd be as sore as sore could be.

"I'm saying there are too many pieces. Madi is framed for Loraine's murder. Then the body is torched and the coroner killed. Then we have two men who attack us and want the truth about Loraine from Madi. Then we find out that the body wasn't even Loraine at all but Kathy Smart. Fast-forward a few days and suddenly Miller decides to take her after we found the place that Kathy was most likely killed? Then I run into Ray, who has this album? And Loraine doesn't know where Madi is?"

Julian leaned across the table to the photo album. He tapped his index finger on the cover.

"Why did they bother taking this from my car? When did they even do it? While we were in the woods or after Miller ambushed me? Out of everything *this* confuses me the most," he admitted. "Madi said this was boxed away because the memories were too hard. Why on earth would you chance connecting yourself to a kidnapping for someone else's photo album?"

"You wouldn't," Desmond finally said. "Not unless it was important."

He moved toward the album and took the chair in front of it. Wordlessly he opened it and began to examine each picture. His brothers weren't as worried about it. Declan shook his head.

"I can only work with the facts I have on hand," he said. "And those are that Miller knocked you out and Madi is gone. Then Loraine and Ray attacked you and disappeared. We need more information." He turned to Caleb and Detective Santiago. "Jazz, I need you to go talk to Nathan Wilson again. I know he alibied out for Kathy Smart's murder but since we've seen Loraine alive, maybe he'll have more to say. Caleb, I need you to find out everything you can on Ray, start-

ing with another thorough pass over the cabin."
Both nodded. "As for me, I'm going to dig deep
into Detective Miller. Des, stay with Julian and
work the photo album angle."

The sheriff put his hat back on. Everyone
agreed on their jobs. Everyone but Julian. He followed the sheriff out to the front porch.

"Declan," he called. "I want to help. I can't do
that with a photo album from the past."

Declan's expression softened. He clapped a
hand on Julian's shoulder.

"You ran about ten miles today in a storm, hurt
and bound, just to sound the alarm. In the last
week alone you have fought off attackers while
trying your damnedest to keep Madi safe."

"And Miller got her anyway," Julian said.

Declan shook his head.

"He was supposed to be a good guy," he replied.
"They're the worst kind of bad. The ones we never
see coming." He dropped his hand and adjusted
his hat. The rain had stopped but his hat was still
dark from it. "Let the people who live here scour
the county while you help Desmond. If we come
at this thing from enough angles we'll eventually
find Madi in the middle."

Julian didn't want to, but he nodded in agree-
ment. The sheriff didn't waste any more time. He
took off along with the detectives. Julian went

back into the house and pulled a chair up next to Desmond.

"How much did Madi tell you about her past?" he asked without looking up from the page of pictures he was currently on. "About our past?"

"Everything."

"Even Andrés Casas?"

Julian nodded.

"The boy she hurt at recess," he supplied. That garnered a look from Desmond.

"The boy she hurt at recess," he repeated as confirmation. "As far as I know she's never told anyone that story before. At least no one outside therapy and those group functions we all went to." He gave Julian a small smile. "She must really care about you to open up like that." Julian couldn't deny that made him feel good, but he knew there was no time for it. Desmond looked back to the photo album but continued.

"You know, I've always told her that there's no shame in what she did to Andrés. She was a kid who had been through a trauma and hadn't had the right tools to process it yet. That's why Ma was so excited for Madi when she went to that camp thing with children who had been through traumas. She wanted Madi to see that she wasn't alone." He stopped on the page with the group shot of the children, Madi in the front, arms crossed and smiling.

"She said she turned around toward the end of it."

Desmond nodded.

"Yeah. The first few meetings weren't that great. A few kids tried to make friends with her and she roasted them. Ma got a call about it. Then they sat down and after that Madi got better."

"Roasted?"

Desmond tapped the face of a boy and girl a few kids down from Madi.

"I'm not proud of it but Caleb and I overheard Ma and Madi talking about it. Apparently they were making fun of some of the kids and she went off on them. I mean, she said some really nasty stuff." Desmond shrugged. "I'm sure I would have done the same, to be honest."

They lapsed into silence as Desmond went through the rest of the album. Julian looked over his shoulder, trying to see if an objective pair of eyes could see something family couldn't.

Neither had any success.

"These are mostly just us as kids," Desmond said, pushing the album away in frustration. "I don't know why they would take it. Unless it was by accident? It's just such a personal thing to take. I mean, I'm surprised Madi even took it out of the loft and *she's* in it."

Julian straightened in his chair.

"That's it," he said, a thought hitting him like a lightning bolt.

"What?"

He grabbed the album and started to flip through it in earnest.

"What is it?" Desmond asked again.

Julian didn't want to get either of their hopes up until he was sure.

"It's just a thought," he said, skimming each page quickly. When he came to the end of the album his adrenaline spiked. "These pictures should only mean something to the people in them." He flipped to the middle and slid the album to Desmond. "I know it's a stretch but what if Loraine or Ray or both are in one?"

Desmond looked down at the group picture. He shook his head but didn't say no.

"Wouldn't Madi have recognized them or their names? They were guests at her inn. She talked to them at length."

"Why else would they grab the album? They look about the same age. Honestly, how hard is it to look completely different from when you were ten? I've seen people from high school who have had to remind me who they are, and that was a lot more recent than elementary school." Julian stood and reached across the table to Desmond's phone. He handed it to the man. "It may be one heck of a stretch but why don't we start with the two kids that you say hated Madi?"

Desmond took the phone.

"I'll call Caleb," he decided. "I mean, what have we got to lose?"

Julian knew it didn't need to be said out loud but he couldn't help it.

"If we can't find her? Everything."

Chapter Twenty-One

Only one man came into the room. It did little to calm Madi's nerves.

"Nice to see you again, Blondie."

He wore a smirk that was nowhere near charming. It was the man with the gun. The one who had chased them across the roof, shooting. Now that she could focus her attention on him and not escaping, Madi noted that his eyes were an alarming shade of green. Like they were radioactive. It was hard to look away from them. Green Eyes seemed amused as he dragged a metal chair through the doorway and across the room. He set it down in front of Madi with a widening grin and unbuttoned the bottom of his blazer.

"Last time we didn't get a chance to talk," he said, taking a seat. He was so close their knees nearly touched. "Let's do something about that now."

Madi shared a quick look with the detective. She felt more fear than she wanted to admit.

"Who are you?" Madi asked, careful to add a tremble to her voice. She and Miller hadn't gotten out of their restraints, but they had managed to make a plan. One that relied on her acting skills. She just wanted to get as many answers as she could first.

Stalling *was* the name of the game after all.

"I'm asking the questions," he skirted. "Starting with your involvement with Loraine Wilson's disappearance."

Well, that hadn't worked, Madi thought with disdain.

"My involvement with Loraine starts and stops with her being a guest at my inn. I didn't even make the reservation with her. I talked to Nathan's assistant. I don't know what happened to Loraine."

"You called and had her phone before she disappeared," he countered. "There was a dead woman in your bed who looked just like Loraine."

Madi had a hard time keeping her anger in check. Her frustration.

"I don't know how, but someone made that call from my phone. Not me. I was just as surprised as anyone to find that woman. I have no clue what's going on. Honestly, I thought it was you and your friend who were behind it after you came to the inn."

The man shook his head.

"If we wanted to kill someone, it wouldn't be

as messy as all of this." He motioned around the room. "I'm just here for answers, and I don't believe for a second you don't have them. All fingers point to you on this one, Madeline Nash." Green Eyes reached into the inner pocket of his blazer. "Speaking of fingers."

He pulled out a handful of what looked like paper straws. Why paper straws, she wondered.

"She doesn't know anything," Miller ground out, pulling up against his restraints. "You can't make her talk about what she doesn't know."

That was when Madi realized the man was holding bamboo skewers. They were short but their pointed ends were enough to make fear roar through her.

"They say torture doesn't work," the man said, nonchalantly rolling the sticks between his hands. "But I don't think of what I do as torture. That's such an ugly word. What *I* do I view as more of an incentive plan. I ask a question and then give you a really good incentive to give an answer."

He put the skewers on the bench next to her but kept one in his hand. Madi tried to move as far away from him and it as she could but her hands could only go so far. He grabbed the fingers of her left hand, flattening the back of her hand completely against the bench. In his other hand he held the one skewer.

"So let's get to the incentive," he said. "To keep

this wooden skewer from going under your fingernail I want you to tell me what you did to Loraine and where she is now."

Miller started to really struggle against his restraints. Madi didn't hear what he was saying. Her vision blurred. Fear and panic were slowly consuming her. Being threatened by a gun was terrifying, but unless you'd been shot before, it was hard to imagine the pain of being on the receiving end of bullet. But something going under her fingernail? Something being pushed into her skin? That was a pain she could already feel. It turned her blood cold and at the same time made her sweat.

It also made stalling harder.

She opened her mouth but didn't know what to say.

Then Miller spoke. He didn't look at Madi as he did so.

"We can take you to Loraine. But you'll need both of us to get to her."

The man twirled the skewer in his hand. He narrowed his gaze on the detective before moving it to Madi. She nodded to confirm the lie.

"Is she alive?" he asked.

"She is," Miller said before Madi could make a sound. "She's just hard to get to unless you know exactly where she is. That's why we didn't say anything. You don't stand a chance to find her without us."

"Without you two," Green Eyes deadpanned. "You're not working together. You hate each other."

"It's the perfect cover," Madi interjected. "Who would ever suspect?"

He kept twirling that skewer around. Every movement terrified her.

Finally he stopped.

"Fine. I'll bite." He let go of her hand and put the skewers back into his inner blazer pocket. He went to the door and stopped. As if it was a playful afterthought he looked over his shoulder. He was nothing but smug. "I should warn you, if you're lying, the incentives only become more enticing. So is there anything you'd like to add?"

Despite her fear, Madi surprised herself.

"If Nathan hadn't outsourced his dirty work we would have all been fine."

Green Eyes continued to stare.

Madi worried she'd lipped off to the wrong person. However, he finally snorted.

"It's always the damaged ones who cause all the trouble," he said. He left, shutting the door tight behind him.

Then they were alone with their lie.

DOROTHY NASH HANDED her revolver to Julian in secret.

"I follow the law," she said in an almost whisper. "My husband was law, my children are law and I respect it. I also know that look in your eye and know that we both understand sometimes laws can be broken for the greater good." She placed her hand on his and dropped her voice even lower. Desmond was out on the porch talking to someone on the phone. Through the open kitchen window Julian couldn't hear exactly what he was saying but his body language was loud enough that he got the gist.

New information had come through the wire and it wasn't good.

"Madi and I have butted heads time and time again but it's only because we're both stubborn, stubborn women," she continued. "That baby of hers, of *yours*, will no doubt be the same way. So it's best if you know now that there isn't anything my stubbornness wouldn't do for them. You get both of our babies home, okay? Whatever it takes. And here…"

Julian checked the gun and put it into the waist-band of his jeans while she hurried out of the room. When she got back there was a Stetson in her hands.

"If it rains again this will help keep it out of your eyes." Julian gave her a small smile and bent down so she could place the cowboy hat atop his head. It was a surprisingly good fit. "Not bad, Mr. Mercer," Dorothy said with approval. "You look just like a local."

"Thank you, Mrs. Nash. I mean it."

"You're family now," she said with a dismissive wave of her hand. "And call me Dorothy."

Julian thanked her again. She embraced him in a hard hug.

"I've already told the boys but I'm going to tell you, too. The moment you hear anything, you let me know. I'll be at Desmond's with Nina, Molly and Clive. Everyone else who works on the ranch has been ordered to stay home until those awful people are caught."

"Will do."

Dorothy's body language was rigid, worry slowly crushing her. Julian felt the same weight against him. Since pitching their theory about the photo album to Declan, twenty minutes had passed. Waiting had been one of the hardest things Julian had ever had to do. If Dorothy hadn't come in for an update at the same time Desmond had gotten the call, Julian would have pressed his ear against Desmond's phone if he'd had to just to hear what was going on.

Julian hurried outside, checking to make sure the gun was secure again, and stopped next to Desmond with his heart in his throat. The Nash triplet kept his expression blank. He held up his finger.

"Fine," he said to the person on the other line. "Yeah. I get it... All right. Bye."

Desmond was angry. That much was clear. But he wasn't devastated. It was the only thing that kept Julian's mouth shut until the man explained himself.

"I can't believe it but you might have been right about Loraine and Ray being those kids in the picture," he started. "At least, they weren't always who they say they were."

"Let me guess, their real names aren't Loraine and Ray?"

"They are," Desmond corrected. "But they weren't always. Loraine apparently had her name changed five years ago, according to Nathan's assistant. Though she didn't know what the previous name was. Jazz is looking into that now. As for Ray, nothing on him has been found. Nothing. Zilch. He didn't start popping up until three years ago when he got a job on a construction crew. Caleb talked to his boss briefly. He said all he knew about Ray was he had a serious girlfriend and a nasty scar covered with a tattoo. Caleb is trying to track the girlfriend down now. That's all they've got so far but they're still digging." He sighed. "If they are in one of those pictures in the photo album, we don't have any proof. None of those kids look like them. We might still be grasping at straws here."

It was Julian's turn to hold up his finger to ask for patience. He turned on his heel and went to the dining room. There he grabbed the photo album. He flipped through it as he ran back to the porch.

"Since these pictures are older I'm not surprised that their quality isn't the greatest. That, plus the fact that it's hard to take a picture of a bunch of kids, made me think that this was an error made by human or camera." Julian found the group picture and pointed to a boy near Madi. He moved his finger to focus on the boy's right forearm. His entire arm was partially blurry. He'd moved as the picture was taken. However, there was a dark patch across it that disappeared around the elbow. "But now that you said it, don't you think that could be a nasty scar?"

Desmond bent over the picture.

"Caleb said the scar was on his arm but didn't specify where."

Julian felt another surge of adrenaline waiting in the wings, prickling against his skin and mind. Ready to pounce when the next puzzle piece finally fitted. An excitement he seemed to be sharing with Desmond. His eyes widened.

"We need another picture of him. I know Madi put most of her stuff from back then in the loft but Ma had us sneak some of her old things into the Hidden Hills attic when she moved out there. Maybe there are more pictures there or something else we can use?"

"Or there could be more in the loft," Julian had

to point out. "Madi didn't look through any of the boxes after she found this."

"We need more time!"

Desmond ran a hand over the back of his neck, stressed.

Julian had to agree.

"Why don't you go look through the loft boxes and I'll go to Hidden Hills and look there? There's not much we can do around here other than wait. We might just find something now that we know what to look for."

It didn't take long for Desmond to make up his mind. They floored it to the barn. Desmond hopped out and motioned to the driver's seat.

"There's a key to the inn on the key ring. The one next to the truck key," he said. "Call me if you find anything."

They didn't waste any more time talking. Julian took off toward the inn. Every inch he sped across—every foot, every mile—he thought of no one but Madi and his unborn child.

When he saw Madi again he swore he'd never leave her side.

Hidden Hills had been crawling with lawmen the last two times he'd come to the end of the road. Julian half expected the same this time around. Instead there were only two cars. One was Madi's. They'd been driving his SUV around when needed. The same SUV he hadn't expected to see again. At least not parked outside Hidden Hills.

Yet there it was.

Julian hit the brakes.

He came to Hidden Hills looking for a clue that could lead to Madi. What better one to find than the vehicle that had disappeared along with her?

"WELL, ISN'T THIS FUN?"

Green Eyes was not amused, despite his word choice. Madi was right there with him. Miller, too. The three of them were in varying states of agitation standing in the entryway of Hidden Hills.

"Should I worry about more pink handcuffs?" he added, eyeing the stairs.

"Not unless that's your thing," Madi shot back. Her fear of torture had taken a momentary back seat. She hated being afraid in her own home.

Miller bumped her shoulder. The well-dressed man snorted.

"My *thing* is making difficult people tell me what I want to know." He dragged his eyes back to hers and smiled sweetly. "And making them pay when they lie to me. Are you going to be one of those people, Blondie?"

"I already told you, I need a key from upstairs before we do anything else." It was a lie. One she and Miller had cobbled together in the minute or so they'd been alone on the bench. Their goal was to create as many possibilities of escape, while also rolling the dice that they'd run into someone who could help them.

Madi had refused to lie about the ranch, as Miller had originally wanted. The man may have had bamboo skewers but that didn't mean he wasn't also carrying a gun. She wasn't going to chance Nathan and his men happening upon her family or the workers on the ranch who might as well have been family.

Now, though, Madi felt like the circle around them was tightening. No one was at the inn and Madi didn't know how to keep Green Eyes's attention without being subjected to torture.

And she had to pee again, if she was being honest.

"Hey, Cap, how does it look up there?" Green Eyes yelled up the stairs. His partner, who had surprisingly kept his distance from them, appeared on the steps. He wasn't as well dressed as his counterpart. Instead he had on a graphic tee of a band Madi hadn't heard of along with a pair of gray cargo pants. Those pockets looked weighted. Madi was afraid to know what he was carrying in them.

"I checked everywhere. No one's up there," Cap said, annoyed. "I'll take her up and you and the badge can make sure no one sneaks up on us here."

Madi's stomach twisted at the suggestion. Green Eyes might have been terrifying but there was something about Cap that made her skin crawl.

"Oh, so *he's* the boss," Miller said at her side. He chuckled. "I was trying to figure out the dynamic but I get it now."

Cap snickered; his partner did not.

"Laugh it up, old man. I wonder if you'll still be this funny when I start carving into you for lying. You do anything and I'll gut her." Madi yelped as Green Eyes grabbed the back of her shirt and pushed her to the stairs. "I'll take them both up. Cap, you keep watch."

Miller fell in line with a grunt. Madi's mind was racing. While there was a key to her post office box in a desk upstairs, it wasn't going to magically make Nathan's men let her and Miller go. She didn't know how long it would even help them stall. What lie could she tell to save them?

There was another key to where Loraine really was in the PO box?

Madi wouldn't have believed it. She doubted the man at her side would, either.

"It's in my room," she said when he paused at the second-floor landing. The three of them shuffled into her living suite. The door leading into her bedroom was splintered. No thanks to the man next to her.

"You aren't leaving through the window this time," he warned once they were inside.

Madi's legs started to shake. Her bluff was failing. She shared a look with Miller. He knew it was about to get bad, too. He cut his eyes around the room and then back to the man. Green Eyes was watching them both with a grin.

"What seems to be the problem?" He crossed his arms and stopped in front of them. He was so cocky. So smug. He was a man who was used to getting what he wanted. By force. No matter if his prey was innocent or not.

No matter if they were carrying a child or not.

The walk-in closet door was open behind him. The key she had alluded to was in her jewelry box inside.

Yet by the look in his eye, Madi already knew how that would play out. There was no lie she could tell to convince him to continue the wild-goose chase. He'd hurt her. He'd hurt Miller. Then Cap would join in.

They wouldn't stand a chance.

Julian.

She missed out on her chance to get to know him the last several months because she'd been afraid to let anyone in. Now? Now it was a regret that rivaled her fear of the unknown.

Not only did Madi want to continue to get to know him, she wanted the chance to love him, too. She wanted him to know her and to be loved by him. She wanted their family to grow.

And she wasn't going to let Green Eyes take that away from her without a fight.

"There's no problem," Madi answered. She slowly slid her right foot back to give her better balance. She could feel Miller's eyes on her. Madi hoped his hands being bound wouldn't throw off his survival instincts. "Because I just realized something you probably didn't think to hide."

The man's eyebrow quirked up.

"Oh yeah, what's that?"

Madi's muscles started to vibrate in anticipation. She glanced at Miller. She'd spent most of her life hating him, yet now she felt a kinship. An understanding. Whether or not he knew exactly what she was doing, he gave a small nod.

Madi stilled her nerves. She thought of Julian when she answered.

"I don't think you have a gun."

Miller threw his entire weight into the man. It pushed them both back into the closet. Madi followed, landing a kick to Green Eyes as they hit her hanging clothes.

"Cap," he yelled out. Miller's hands might have been bound but he did fast work of getting the man to the floor. Madi hovered, waiting for an opening. She didn't want to hit Miller and she certainly didn't want the man to get a hit in on her or her stomach.

"Cap!"

"Madi—" Miller grunted, swinging down at the man. "Go—go lock the door!"

Madi turned on her heel and ran for the suite's main door. There were bullet holes in it. The lock was busted. She hadn't noticed that detail before.

Footsteps thundered up the steps.

Madi felt an overwhelming sense of déjà vu as Cap appeared at the top of the stairs with a gun in hand. He pointed it without hesitation. Madi tried to shield her stomach as a gunshot exploded through the house.

She squeezed her eyes shut. Waiting for the pain.

Instead all she felt was the rapid beating of her heart.

Then she heard a thud.

"Madi?" Miller asked, running in behind her. It forced her to open her eyes.

Cap was on the floor. His eyes were open but blood was already pooling around him. Miller bumped up against her shoulder.

"Get back," Miller whispered, easing in front of her. "We don't know who it is."

"Julian?" Madi called, ignoring the detective. Who else would have shot the bad guy?

Red hair ascended the stairs. A red-painted smile followed.

Loraine gave her a wink.

"Don't worry," she cooed. "No one is going to hurt you but me."

Chapter Twenty-Two

Loraine swung the gun around and pulled the trigger. Miller made an awful noise. He stumbled backward into Madi. She barely managed to keep standing as his weight hit her side.

"Miller!"

"Get out of here," he yelled.

Loraine laughed. Madi grabbed the man's arm and pulled.

"Come on," she said hurriedly.

Miller didn't fight her but he did struggle. Together they barely made it back into her bedroom.

"He might have a phone," Madi realized, looking at Green Eyes in the closet. He was motionless against the floor.

Miller didn't respond. Madi went from pulling him along to pushing him. It wasn't gentle by any means but she wanted a door between them and Loraine. The closet was their best bet. Especially if it meant they could get the man's cell phone.

"Oh, Madi. Going in there isn't going to stop

me," Loraine called from the bedroom doorway. She was taking her sweet time.

Miller hit the ground and crawled out of the way so Madi could close the door behind him. An antique glider her mother had given her when she'd found out Madi was pregnant sat in the corner. Madi dragged it in front of the door, heart beating a million miles per second.

It blocked the door but it wouldn't hold for long.

Madi knelt down and went through her would-be torturer's pockets. Desperate for a phone. All she found instead were the skewers and a knife she would have preferred to never think about again. However, it was their only weapon.

"You've got to be kidding me," she cried.

"Get away from the door," Miller said before his words devolved into coughing.

Madi joined him against the wall directly to the left of the door. Miller's gunshot wound was gut-wrenching. He'd been hit in chest. Blood had already soaked his shirt. Madi grabbed one of her T-shirts hanging above him and knelt next to him. It was an awkward movement with her belly. She tipped over to the ground and decided sitting was the only option if she wanted to help the detective.

"Put pressure on this," she ordered, handing him the shirt. "I need to be ready if she comes in."

"Oh, Madi, what are you really going to do?" Loraine asked through the door. Madi tightened her grip around the knife's handle. "I know you, baby girl, you're not that kind of gal. You let your words do the cutting, right? The rest of us are the ones who use the blades."

"I don't know what you're talking about, Loraine," Madi volleyed back. "I don't even know why you're here."

The door shook but never opened. Madi put both of her hands around the knife's handle. She was shaking.

"I really am going to have to thank Dr. Pulaski," Loraine said through the door. "When she said she could really make me look unrecognizable she wasn't kidding."

Madi shared a confused look with Miller. His face had become pale.

Loraine laughed.

"I guess you're confused, huh?" she continued. "Don't worry, that was the point. I would have been upset if you'd figured out who I was."

Madi shook her head, as if that would knock loose some answers.

"Who are you?"

Loraine's cackle was so loud it was like she was inches from them and not on the other side of the wall.

"Does Tabitha Walker ring a bell or did I fail to leave an impression?"

Madi felt like her world flipped upside down.

She lowered the knife, eyes as wide as they would go.

"Who?" Miller whispered.

Madi shook her head, refusing to believe it.

"Answer him, Madi," Tabitha called out. "Tell him who I am!"

Madi's mouth had gone dry. When she spoke it was like sandpaper.

"A girl who hated me more than you ever did."

Tabitha laughed again.

"That's right! You aren't the only one, Detective Miller, who has dibs on cursing Madi Nash's name! That's actually why I had to shoot you. See, I need you to die so I can put it on Madi and then I need Madi to die so I can put it on my husband, who I will then take out in self-defense. My God, what a wild cycle this has become!"

Madi felt like she was going to be sick. Even more so when the door shook violently. "But I'd like to see your face for some of this, Madi! Open the door or I'll have to go get Cooper to help me."

"Oh no, no, no." Madi put a hand over her mouth. She squeezed her eyes shut. "No, no, no."

"What?" Miller asked. It sounded like he tried to move closer. He sucked in a breath. She met his stare.

"She's just realized how royally screwed she is," Tabitha answered. "I'll be right back! Time to tell Cooper the inn is secure enough and it's to come up! Don't go anywhere!"

"Why are you screwed? Who are these people?" Miller prodded.

Madi cradled her stomach. She took a deep, wavering breath.

"Tabitha Walker and Cooper Tosh. I went to a therapy camp of sorts when I was younger for kids who had been through traumas. They were in my group." She shook her head, remembering how the two had rubbed her the wrong way even as a child. "They were mean, vindictive. Used their anger to hurt anyone and everyone they could. One day they did awful things to one of the boys in the same group and I—well, I humiliated them in front of everyone. Used *my* anger as an excuse to cause more pain. After it happened, I turned over a new leaf, but they were pulled from the group before the next session. But that was so long ago. I actually hadn't even thought of them until earlier today." Madi laughed. It was a hollow sound even to her ears. "How's that for a coincidence?"

Miller tried to sit up straighter. The shirt he was using for pressure was completely drenched.

"You need to get out of here," he said. "Make it to the window and repeat what you and Julian did the other night along the roof."

"I'm not leaving you," Madi decided. "By taking that bullet you saved me and I'm not—"

"And by leaving me you can save your daughter."

Madi opened her mouth only to close it again. Miller's expression softened. He was right. It wasn't just her she was trying to save.

She had to think of her child.

Miller must have seen the decision in her expression. He smiled.

"Godspeed, Madeline Nash."

Madi took the knife, moved the chair and threw open the closet door. She ran across the room without hesitation. Then it was another bout of déjà vu. A gunshot went off somewhere in the house behind her. Madi didn't wait to see who caused or received it. She needed to get back to the trellis and head for the woods. Julian would find her. She just knew it.

Madi used the palms of her hands to push the window up. The knife's blade tapped against the glass. It made the urgency of her escape grow.

Loraine had gone from stuck-up stranger with a mean streak to a vengeful specter from her past. Neither had cared about the child in Madi's stomach.

"I was about to worry that you weren't going to try to run. Though, I assure you, I'm not like my husband's lackeys," came a voice behind her. Tabitha had never gone to get Cooper at all. "I'm not about to go racing across the roof when a well-placed bullet can save me the work." Madi stopped midmovement. Slowly she turned, knife out in front of her. "I have work to do," Tabitha continued, standing in the doorway of the bedroom. She still had her gun. "And I'll be damned if I'm going to let you make it any harder than you already have."

Tabitha's voice was unforgiving. So was her expression. It twisted with anger.

"I don't understand," Madi admitted. "Why did you come here? What's your endgame? Why now? Have you really hated me this long?"

Tabitha shook her gun at the knife and then motioned to the bed. Madi suddenly felt exhausted. She dropped her weapon and perched on the edge of her bed. Now she was directly across from the woman. It seemed to satisfy her.

"You're putting yourself right back into the center of attention again," she started. "I'm not surprised. Thinking you're the cause of all of this *and* the endgame. Just like when we were kids, here you are clawing for attention. Making everything about you. You think your words back then could cause all of this?" She took a small step forward, nostrils flared and lips thinned. "Despite popular opinion, you aren't that good."

"Then why?" Madi asked, frustration nearly boiling over. So many questions, still not enough answers. "What are you really doing here? And how does Cooper fit into it? How does your husband? Why kill Kathy Smart?"

The corner of Tabitha's mouth twitched. Madi could only assume she was gearing up for another show of cruel disregard for basic decency.

"It's quite simple, really. Even after your boy toy showed up and ruined our original plan." She moved to the end of the bed. Madi wondered if she was like a Bond villain. Would the need to share her diabolical plan outweigh the need to keep her plan in forward motion?

Tabitha licked her lips. She smiled.

"Love," she said simply.

That caught Madi off guard.

"Love? You have a funny way of showing it for your husband."

Tabitha's smile vanished.

"Cooper is the one I love. The only thing I love about my husband is his money," she said. "Which is why I needed to die before I disappeared. You can't suspect a dead person of taking your money, now can you?"

"That's why you killed Kathy Smart. You needed everyone to think you were dead so you used that poor woman's body," Madi realized. "Then—what?—you decided to set me up for it and leave when I was convicted for it?"

Tabitha shook the gun, anger lighting up her features again.

"Don't make it sound that simple," she yelled. "We thought of everything. Everything! For years we looked for the perfect plan to make our escape so we could live out our days with the money I'd been collecting in secret. All that we needed was a fall guy. One we could set up perfectly. It wasn't until a lovely man approached us in a bar that I realized we could get what we wanted *and* knock down Overlook's beloved Madi Nash. You owning an isolated bed-and-breakfast? Well, that just made everything easier. Cooper even spent time up here months ago, watching, to confirm you were basically all alone. He became so good at sneaking around that he took it to the ranch and managed to stumble onto your tree house! He only got better, too. When we actually started to execute our plan, it was flawless! Taking your phone to call mine while you were distracted before you even went up to your room and then putting the body and shotgun in their places? All while you were in the bath? Perfect."

"But things got messy when Julian showed up, didn't they?" Another piece of the puzzle fell into place. "And let me guess, you didn't know about Kathy Smart's metal plate with a registration number. You didn't count on your husband hiring people to find out the truth, either, did you?"

Tabitha snarled.

"It doesn't matter what happened. We keep

adapting." Tabitha nodded to the closet. "This crime scene will confuse everyone so much they won't think about me until we're long gone. Sure, it's not as ideal as the original plan of playing dead, but like I said, we keep adapting."

The sound of something heavy hitting the ground below them vibrated the house. Tabitha's eyes widened but she didn't say anything. Instead she pulled the gun up to aim at Madi's head, and for the first time since they'd started talking, Tabitha looked down at Madi's stomach. Her expression didn't soften. There was no remorse in her eyes when she returned her gaze.

"Please, Tabitha. Please don't do this," Madi pleaded. "You and Cooper, just go. Right now. Let me call in that Miller has been shot and the response will create an opening for the two of you to get out of town. You don't have to do this."

"I'd do anything to ensure our future. Anything."

Madi had never known fear so acute. It consumed her. She hunched over, absurdly hoping she could protect her child somehow. Pain squeezed her heart. She closed her eyes.

"Funny, I was thinking the same thing."

Madi's head flew up, her heart already singing.

Julian stood behind Tabitha. He had a gun to her head.

"If you hurt her, your guy, the one I just hurt

very badly downstairs, dies," he said, voice so low and dangerous that goose bumps erupted across Madi's skin. "Give me the gun and he lives. Simple as that."

Tabitha opened her mouth to say something. She thought better of it. Julian slowly circled her, gun revolving around her head, until he was the one looking her in the eye.

"I should warn you. It will take a lot more than some bullets to keep me from protecting them."

Madi couldn't see Tabitha's face anymore but she heard the defeat in the sigh that followed. She threw her gun onto the bed. Madi scooped it up.

"Now, make sure Cooper doesn't die," Tabitha spit.

"I already did. I'm guessing most, if not all, of the law enforcement from Wildman County are almost here."

Julian ordered her to the closet, where he used Madi's belts to restrain her and Green Eyes. Sirens blared in the distance. Madi dropped down to Miller's side. He was unconscious but alive. She put pressure against his wound but looked up at Julian, standing sentry in the doorway.

Without the threat of a gun pointed at her, Madi took in new, terrifying details. He was bruised and bloodied, his clothes ripped and stained. However, the most alarming detail was the bullet wound in his side.

"Julian, you've been shot!"

The man, the beautiful father of her child, simply smiled.

"I wasn't lying. Nothing was going to keep me from you two. Not even bullets."

Chapter Twenty-Three

Chance Montgomery picked up the cowboy hat off the hospital nightstand and gave it an appraising look.

"Not bad," he said. "Not my particular style, but have you seen me?" He grinned. "You can't copy something *this* good."

Julian laughed. It hurt, but nowhere near as bad as it had before surgery. Now it was more of a soreness. A bullet to the side could have been a lot worse. Thankfully, Cooper Tosh had been a poor shot.

"Yeah, yeah, we get it. You're God's gift to mankind. Now, why don't you help me carry my stuff out of here?"

Chance laughed and put Julian's bag across his shoulder. Julian grabbed the cards that had been set up on the table in his room and both of them looped a vase of flowers under each arm. By the time they made it down to Chance's truck, they looked like they'd robbed a florist.

"I guess the town of Overlook has decided they believe you and Madi are the good guys." Chance threw the bag in the back and put his flowers on the seat between them. It was a crowded but colorful space in the small cab.

"Yep. Turns out Tabitha's love for Cooper wasn't just a dramatic declaration. She cut a deal and told the cops everything in an attempt to reduce his sentence. She owned up to killing the coroner, shooting Holloway and shooting Cooper's girlfriend, Kathy Smart." Julian shrugged.

"You don't think she did those things?"

"I think she did them, I just think she didn't do them alone. But I get it," Julian admitted. "She's trying to protect someone she loves. I know the feeling." Julian cut a look over to Chance. After he'd gotten out of surgery Chance had been in his hospital room along with Madi. She'd called the cowboy in and given him the lowdown on everything that had happened. Chance had been in town every day since, trying to help where he could.

He was a great friend. Which was why Julian had to apologize.

"When the cops checked my alibi and called you, you backed me up. I shouldn't have put you in that situation. Not after everything you've done for me. I'm sorry, Chance. I really am."

The Alabama cowboy took his hand off the steering wheel to wave off the concern.

"I trust you, even the lies you tell," he said. "You believed in Madi and I believed in you. That's no biggie in my book."

"Still, thank you for it."

"No problem."

They drove straight to the ranch and up to the main house. A thrill of nerves went through Julian. Neither man got out of the truck.

"Whatever happened to Nathan, by the way?" Chance finally asked. "I meant to ask but time kept flying by at the bed-and-breakfast with those Nash brothers. They're good at fixing bullet holes and broken things, but, man, when we got to talking about football, it was like the rest of the world went away."

Julian laughed at that. The Nash brothers hadn't been the only ones pitching in to help with the damage that had been done to Hidden Hills and the ranch. Overlook wasn't just a town, it was a community. One that was quick to act. Madi's bed had already been replaced with a new mattress before Julian was even out of surgery.

"Last I heard he was still paying a fortune for a lawyer who wasn't doing a great job. I don't think anyone can save him from prison. He hired hit men to torture a pregnant woman and a lawman. Not to mention everything Tabitha added to it. Telling the FBI about all of his seedy business dealings definitely didn't do him any favors."

"And to think, he had no clue his wife had only married him to steal his money, fake her own death and run off with her boyfriend." Chance shook his head. "If Tabitha had just tried to run off without all the killing she might have made it. Instead she managed to go up against two separate parties all looking and fighting for the truth."

"Yep," Julian agreed. "My favorite part of this whole mess, and please note my sarcasm as I say *favorite*, has to be what went down with the photo album."

"What do you mean? When you found the group picture of the kids?"

Julian shook his head, still having a hard time believing what he said next.

"Right after Miller showed up at the trail and the three of us went to the tree house, Nathan's lackeys parked and went into the woods after us for the ambush. While we were in the woods Ray, aka Cooper, broke into my SUV and grabbed the photo album."

"How did he know you had it? Was he following you two?"

"Bingo. After he ran into us at the stable he apparently decided to keep an eye on us and use the excuse that he was just on the ranch as a guest if caught. That's what Tabitha said at least."

"So when he saw you with the photo album he decided he needed to take it just in case?"

"Tabitha told him to. She remembered them all taking pictures during camp when they were kids," Julian said. Then he shook his head a little, still in a weird kind of awe with how everything had panned out. "So, while Nathan's hired helpers followed Miller to get to Madi and had us in the woods, Tabitha had her partner in crime follow the photo album. How Cooper didn't see Nathan's men and vice versa is still mind-blowing. It's almost like some kind of slapstick comedy where the audience sees all the near misses but the characters never realize just how close everything came to intersecting."

Chance shook his head. He let out a long whistle.

"This was all just one heck of a mess, if you ask me."

"You got that right, brother." Julian looked at his watch. They still had a little time. "All right, we need to get these inside and then get going. You still up for it?"

Chance laughed. It was from the belly.

"Am *I* up for it? The question is, are you?"

Julian gave his friend a big smile.

"I've never been ready for anything more than I am now."

MADI RAN A hand over her stomach. It wouldn't be long before Addison would make her appearance.

Madi's early worries of being a mother felt like a memory from long ago. Now all she wanted to do was hold her daughter and tell her how much she had been loved before she had ever even taken a breath.

A knock sounded on the door. Madi started to duck into the bathroom when a man's voice floated through.

"It's Miller," he called. "I was wondering if I could have a quick moment."

Madi's already-fluttering nerves slowed again. "Come in!"

Christian Miller was in his Sunday best. He'd even donned a weathered cowboy hat. He took it off when he saw her and placed it against his chest.

"You look nice," he greeted, shutting the door behind them. Madi smiled.

"You don't look so bad, either. Especially for a man who needed two surgeries and should really be following the doctor's orders to stay off your feet."

Miller shrugged.

"What can I say, I'm a stubborn old man." He winced as he moved but Madi decided not to push it. Miller had tried and succeeded to protect her when it counted. He deserved to not be pestered. Plus, whatever had gotten him up the stairs must have been important. His demeanor shifted from pleasant to serious in a heartbeat.

"I know this probably isn't the best time to tell you this, but, well, I think you deserve to know."

"Know what?"

He took an uncertain step forward and dived in.

"Why your father thought I was involved with your abduction all those years ago." Madi hadn't expected that. "You see, when your dad started suspecting that the attacker had connections to the police force, he questioned everyone in the department at length. When he got to me, I lied about where I was and he knew it." A look of clear shame came across his expression. "When I was young I wasn't a good man. Not when it came to my wife. The day you were attacked and taken I'd been with a woman who wasn't my wife. I didn't want anyone to find out. Your dad saw that dishonesty and never let up. It turned everyone's attention on me until, finally, I admitted the truth." He let out a long breath and gave her a small smile filled with regret. "I never blamed your dad for questioning me. I blamed him for putting me in the spotlight. Even though it was my own fault."

"I—I never knew that."

"Because when your dad realized the truth he promised not to tell. But you know how secrets in this town work. Some found out, including my wife." He sighed again. Then he was back to standing tall. "I just wanted to let you know that your dad was a good man. It was me who messed up and it's been me I've been mad at all these years. I never really hated you or your family. Just my idiot younger self. I'm sorry for how I've acted. I really am."

Madi closed the distance between them and hugged the man, careful to be gentle.

"Thank you, Detective," she said at his shoulder. "That means a lot."

Miller returned the hug and then stepped back. He put his cowboy hat back on and cleared his throat.

"Well, now that that's out of the way, I think I'll go find my seat. I'm sure Declan will be here any second now to get you."

He gave her one more smile and left Madi alone again. She didn't know if it was the pregnancy hormones or what, but her eyes started to mist over. When Declan arrived no more than a minute later, his eyes widened in worry.

"I'm okay," she said hurriedly, swatting away his concern. "I'm just—well, I'm just so *happy* and it feels weird."

Declan chuckled.

"That's good, right?"

Madi nodded and took his outstretched arm.

"It's great," she said. "And I have a feeling it's only going to get better."

Declan smiled. While she had a special bond with her triplet brothers, she couldn't deny that the sibling love she felt for her older brother was fierce. He squeezed her hand as if to say it was mutual.

They walked down to the back door that led to Hidden Hills' patio. The blinds were all drawn but Madi could hear the music perfectly when her song started.

"In a different situation, I would point out that this is all happening so fast," Declan said, hand resting on the doorknob. "But somehow it doesn't feel right to say it here. Not with the two of you." Those nerves started to dance across Madi's chest and stomach. "He really loves you and you really love him, don't you?"

Madi nodded.

"I do."

Declan laughed.

"Then wait a few minutes and say that again."

He opened the door and all Madi saw was the man she loved standing at the end of a path of petals, dressed in a suit and smiling at her. Their friends and family stood on either side of the path, but Madi saw only Julian.

The memory of his proposal would forever be branded on her heart.

"You told me that your dad used to say that there's never enough time to do everything, so focus on the one thing you can do," Julian had said from his hospital bed. He'd pulled a ring from beneath his pillow. Madi would later find out he'd asked his mother to bring his grandmother's ring with her when she came to see them. Julian had held the ring up with a smile that she knew would never fade. "And I told you that I thought it was great advice. I still believe that. So I'm going to follow it and do the only thing in this world I think is worth doing." He'd used his other hand to tuck a strand of her hair behind her ear.

"And that is?" she'd asked, nearly breathless.

Julian's smile had only grown.

"Love you," he'd said simply. "You and our family. Forever and always."

Madi had smiled for all she was worth. Just as she was now beneath the wedding arch. That smile was reflected in Julian.

"You may kiss the bride," the preacher exclaimed.

Julian did just that.

"The only thing worth doing," he whispered when the kiss ended.

Madi kept on smiling. She agreed.

"The only thing worth doing."

* * * * *

*Look for more books in Tyler Anne Snell's
Winding Road Redemption miniseries,
coming soon.*

And don't miss the previous book in the series:

Reining in Trouble

Available now from Harlequin Intrigue!

Get 4 FREE REWARDS!

We'll send you 2 FREE Books plus 2 FREE Mystery Gifts.

Harlequin® Romantic Suspense books feature heart-racing sensuality and the promise of a sweeping romance set against the backdrop of suspense.

FREE
Value Over
$20

Get 4 FREE REWARDS!

We'll send you 2 FREE Books
plus 2 FREE Mystery Gifts.

Harlequin Presents® books feature a sensational and sophisticated world of international romance where sinfully tempting heroes ignite passion.

FREE
Value Over
$20